The Gypsy Goddess

MEENA KANDASAMY has published two poetry collections: *Touch* (2006) and *Ms Militancy* (2010). She was a writer-in-residence at the University of Iowa's International Writing Program in 2009, and has since then held visiting fellowships at the Jawaharlal Nehru University in Delhi, the University of Hyderabad, India and at universities in Warwick, Newcastle, Canterbury (UK) and Hong Kong. Her first novel, *The Gypsy Goddess*, was chosen as one of *Independent* newspaper's debuts of the year in 2014 and short-listed/longlisted for several awards including the DSC Prize for South Asian Literature, the International Dylan Thomas Prize, and the Tata Literature Live First Book Award. *The Gypsy Goddess* has been translated into Dutch (Atlas Contact, 2016), German (Wunderhorn Verlag, 2016) and French (Plon, 2017).

Praise for *The Gypsy Goddess*

'Written with an edge and an unflinching eye not frequently encountered in Indian writing in English, Meena uses multiple forms to take the narrative forward. [E]ach one of the chapters has an in-built rhythm that works brilliantly, reading like a poem at times and as reportage at others. Her prose is luminescent and visceral as it devastatingly evokes the horror of people being trampled.'

Anita Nair, *Asian Age*

'For all its humour, for all its dash and sparkle, *The Gypsy Goddess* is a novel chomping at the bit, seething with rage and unafraid to assault the reader with scenes of remorseless rape, cold-blooded revenge killings and the occasional impaled infant. Kandasamy employs cinematic metaphors to devastating effect.... This is a novel whose audacity is matched only by its penchant for shifting register.'

Aditya Mani Jha, *The Sunday Guardian*

'The irreverent disregard for form, the inversions of structure, sentences often pages long, spoken with the frenzy of an eyewitness whose memories run into each other, make her work more poetry than prose. It is from these devices that the almost-magical realism emerges.'

Gayatri Jayaraman, *India Today*

'Kandasamy doesn't just inherit the history of writing about the unspeakable and the forgotten in *The Gypsy Goddess*, she rewrites the novel of violence, and questions every accepted way of turning violence into literature.'

Nilanjana Roy, *Business Standard*

'The poet, novelist, activist and academic Meena Kandasamy is a one-woman, agit-prop literary-political movement. It would take Carol Ann Duffy, Arundhati Roy and, if her first work of fiction

The Gypsy Goddess is anything to go by, Salman Rushdie to match her infinite variety.'

James Kidd, *The Independent*

'Kandasamy's literary sickle takes an angry swipe at class enemies and cultural idols with the same tenacity in this novel as it does in her poems and activism.'

Sudha Tilak, *Business Line*

'The idiom of macho Tamil movie talk – Kandasamy captures perfectly and satirises with her confident and amused mimic's eye.'

Rajni George, *Open Magazine*

'A rambunctious read. This is a book seething with barely banked passion. The author employs a tone in which cynicism is mixed with fury, and to very good use. Fickle as the reader's engagement is anticipated and expected to be, it is imperative that stories such as this be told. Over and over again.'

Deccan Herald

'A rapporteur of the collective conscience, far-removed from all things Orwellian, so real that every page in this book will make you squirm. This is one of the best reportage I have read in a long time of a much-travelled landscape; from the days of Sangam literature and dictums of Thiruvalluvar to Thyagaraja's music, Andal's sweet songs, the words that flow from this land have so far been soft as the kanji, green like the paddy fields. It is marvellous that a young writer has brought the red of the blood into the words on this land.'

Papri Sri Raman, *Book Link*

'Dazzling, maddening, often hilarious … Kandasamy's in-your-face narrative is unashamedly tricksy but handled with sublime confidence.'

Kate Saunders, *The Times*

'One of the standout passages in *The Gypsy Goddess* is the description of the slaughter that unfolds over five pages in a single unflagging and unpunctuated sentence. We want the ordeal to stop but Kandasamy knows that to convey the full force of the horror means keeping a foot on the pedal and intensifying, not abating.'

Malcolm Forbes, *The National*

'This ... novel wears its heart, and politics, on its sleeve and isn't afraid to challenge notions of individualism. It startles, disturbs and agitates.'

***Socialist Review*, UK**

THE GYPSY GODDESS

* * *

Meena Kandasamy

FOURTH ESTATE • *New Delhi*

First published in hardback in India in 2014 by Fourth Estate
An imprint of HarperCollins *Publishers* India

First published in paperback in 2016 by Fourth Estate,
An imprint of HarperCollins *Publishers*

HarperCollins Publishers India, Cyber City, Building 10-A, Gurugram,
Haryana-122002, India
www.harpercollins.co.in

2 4 6 8 10 9 7 5 3 1

P-ISBN: 978-93-5264-027-0
E-ISBN: 978-93-5116-028-1

Printed and bound at
MicroPrints India, New Delhi

MIX
Paper
FSC FSC™ C218906

This product is made of FSC®-certified and other controlled material.

HarperCollins Publishers, Macken House, 39/40 Mayor Street
Upper, Dublin 1, D01 C9W8, Ireland

For Amma, Appa and Thenral
For holding me together

Contents

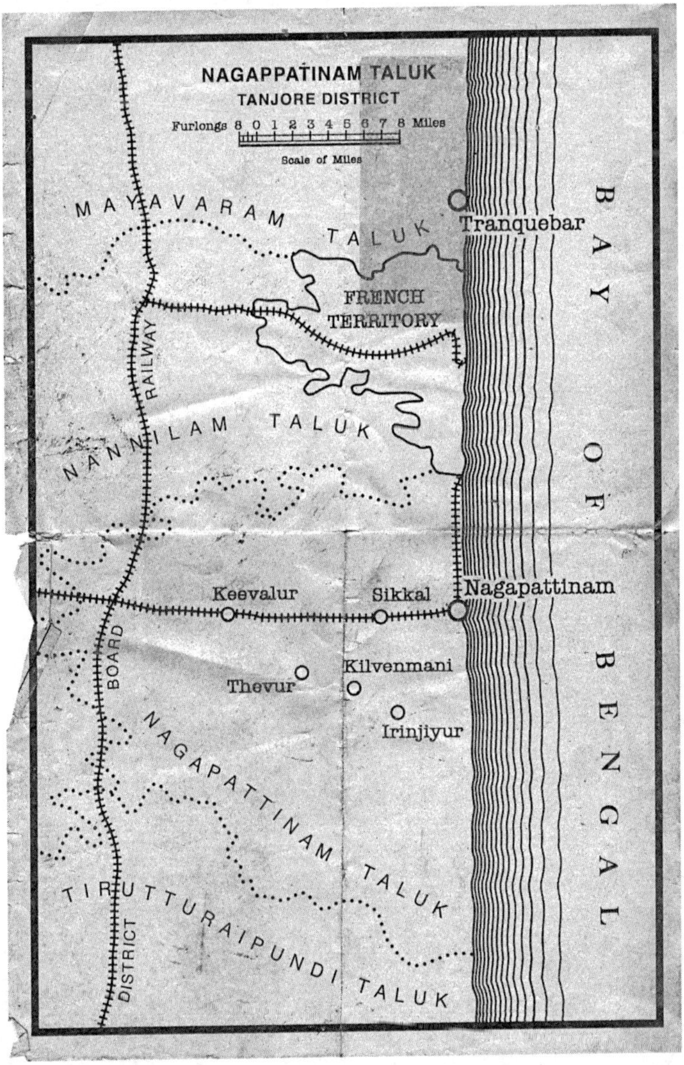
NAGAPPATINAM TALUK
TANJORE DISTRICT
Furlongs 8 0 1 2 3 4 5 6 7 8 Miles
Scale of Miles
MAYAVARAM TALUK
Tranquebar
FRENCH TERRITORY
RAILWAY
NANNILAM TALUK
BAY OF BENGAL
Keevalur
Sikkal
Nagapattinam
BOARD
Kilvenmani
Thevur
Irinjiyur
NAGAPATTINAM TALUK
TIRUTTURAIPUNDI TALUK
DISTRICT

Slaughter and terror did not stop them. How can you frighten a man whose hunger is not only in his own cramped stomach but in the wretched bellies of his children? You can't scare him – he has known a fear beyond every other.

JOHN STEINBECK, *THE GRAPES OF WRATH*

The Gypsy Goddess

PROLOGUE

* * *

Long Live Agriculture! Agriculture Is National Service!!
We Will Increase Paddy Production!
We Will Eradicate Famine!!

PADDY PRODUCERS' ASSOCIATION,
NAGAPATTINAM TALUK
42/2, Mahatma Gandhi Salai, Nagapattinam, Tanjore District

MEMORANDUM SUBMITTED TO THE HONOURABLE CHIEF MINISTER OF MADRAS SEEKING IMMEDIATE REDRESSAL OF THE GRIEVANCES OF PADDY CULTIVATORS

Greetings!

It is with a heavy heart that this petitioner begs to bring to the kind attention of your Honourable Self, some of the sufferings undergone by the paddy cultivators of Nagapattinam as a consequence of the mischievous politics and misconceived propaganda that has gripped the coolies.

For the past ten years, agricultural coolies have been constantly demanding an increase in their daily wages, and whenever it has been denied to them, they have organized strikes and paralysed life in our district. Self-styled Communist leaders, who are themselves comfortably well off, are also responsible for illegal encroachment on other people's lands. Not merely do they disregard the rights of the landowners, but they do so like militant Naxalites, by instigating the labourers to commence farming on these encroached lands. It suffices to state that, in practice, they harvest other people's fields and take away the agricultural produce, a major share of which is given to their leaders.

The increasing agony faced by the landowning *mirasdars* has forced us to create the Paddy Producers Association, and the aim of our organization is twofold: to liberate the agricultural coolies from the wicked company of these dubious leaders; and to create a relationship of mutual goodwill and understanding between the landowners, tenant farmers and the agricultural coolies who play a crucial role in rice cultivation.

The Communist leaders merely keep coming up with a list of demands and inciting their followers to go on strike. When their unreasonable demands are not acceded to, they approach the government, which holds talks between the warring landowners and the labourers, and a temporary settlement is then reached. This petitioner, like other cultivators, is of the opinion that every meeting has extended the privileges of the agricultural coolies and this has empowered and emboldened the Communist leaders, who seek to create famine in order to make this land a fertile breeding ground for Maoism.

This petitioner wishes to point out that in order to

keep creating new agreements, the agricultural coolies keep protesting. All these agreements have been a threat to peace and law and order. Whenever the government officials have decided to hold tripartite talks, these leaders appear with a list of impossible demands. This petitioner, as a landlord from Irinjiyur and being the representative of the *mirasdars*, has remained stubborn and refused to entertain any of these demands, saying that implementation of these demands was impractical, displaying the same tenacity exhibited by the intractable leaders of the opponents. As a consequence of this petitioner's uncompromising stance and his determination not to be held to ransom by a bunch of blackmailing Communists, he has been considered their foremost enemy. They have taken it upon themselves to cause irreparable damage and hardship and, on several occasions, they have threatened to finish off this petitioner and his relatives. Moreover, these verbal threats have often sought to be fructified by carrying out violent agitations outside the petitioner's home. By following his instinct of self-preservation and maintaining a high degree of tolerance to their provocations, the petitioner has managed to safeguard himself from physical harm. However, their immature acts and political tricks have not been successful in shaking either the petitioner's determination or his ideology and, consequently, the desperate Communists have embarked on another shocking and dangerous strategy.

Presently, their leaders have sent away one of their dutiful henchmen named Chinnapillai to some undisclosed location, and they have submitted a complaint that this petitioner killed that man and destroyed all evidence of such a murder. It is reliably learnt that this has been filed as a 'Missing Persons Report' at the Keevalur police station, Nagapattinam, on 15th March 1968 or thereabouts, and this hoax is currently under investigation by the police. At this juncture, it becomes necessary to point out that three years before, a similar conspiracy was hatched to implicate the petitioner. A man named Sannasi went to a village near Karaikkal, and immediately a story started doing the rounds that this man was killed by the landlords. But before this rumour could take the shape of a malicious complaint, it came to be known that Sannasi had died of intoxication from drinking bootleg arrack in that village. The aforementioned complaint exposes the *mala fide* intention of the Communist leaders, who doggedly seek to imprison this petitioner because he presents the greatest threat to their nefarious activities.

Not only have they filed such a complaint, but they have also held public meetings to demand the immediate arrest of this petitioner. Incapable of achieving the expected results in spite of their best efforts, these leaders have changed their plan of attack. As a part of this new strategy, they organize marches close to the petitioner's residence, chant provocative slogans and condemn the petitioner in the most disparaging manner possible. They have rained down curses on him with the secret motive of making him step out of his home so that he could be dealt with in any manner they deemed fit. In such excruciating circumstances, the petitioner cautiously stayed behind bolted doors and saved himself from a miserable fate.

Without a shred of doubt, the petitioner believes that the Communists have identified him as a target of their agitations and that they will succeed in their objective. If the Communists are not made to restrain themselves, and permanent legal measures are not taken to solve this problem, no landlord can remain safe. The petitioner feels that unless this nuisance is nipped in the bud, Nagapattinam is bound to face unprecedented law and order problems.

Although the Communist leaders and the gullible workers who follow them have trespassed on our lands, illegally harvested our crops and caused us immense suffering, we, as the members of the Paddy Producers Association, are committed to a policy of staunch non-violent opposition. To protect ourselves from such routine blackmail and misguided attacks in the future, it has become incumbent upon this petitioner to appeal to your Honourable Self to deliver justice. East Tanjore district is in dire need of protection in order to sustain its honour and tradition of being the granary and rice bowl of the entire land. If the Communists are allowed a free rein, famine is imminent, and it will prove to be calamitous to the people.

In your exemplary book, *Thee Paravattum*, your Honourable Self has written about the fire of reason destroying the dogma of superstitions. Now the time has come to destroy the dogma of communism that has divided the people into classes and set them against each other. If left unchecked, these weeds in our society will choke the hope of any future harvest.

It is respectfully prayed that as the Honourable Chief Minister, Your Excellency shall interfere in this grave matter at the earliest and take necessary steps to restore the lost confidence of the terror-stricken landowners who are living in a constant state of fear, and thereby liberate Nagapattinam from the clutches of Communists in order to prevent violence and bloodshed.

I have the honour of being, Sir,
Your most humble and obedient servant,

Date: 1st May 1968 GOPALAKRISHNA NAIDU
Station: Irinjiyur President

part one

BACKGROUND

* * *

1. *Notes on Storytelling*

It is difficult to write a novel living in a land where despotic bards ensured that for more than a thousand years, literature existed only in the form of poetry – alliteration under the armpit, algebra around the rhyming feet. Meter was all that mattered. But every language put forth its own share of Bacons and banyans and so, Tamil prose was born. A child actor, it made an odd public appearance here and there, every now and then, but the absence of reality TV in those times made a recluse out of this little rebel, who soon refused to speak or sing, and instead opted for solitary confinement. Years later, the first signs of a moustache and breasts began to show, hair sprouted in downward spirals, and prose attained puberty without much fanfare. Riddled with teenage angst and burdened with an androgynous voice, it did not take long for this youngster to realize that poetry could never be replaced. Emerging from a bat-ridden library, the self-sentenced one broke into the system deviously, under the pretext of praise. Copious critical notes on the works of the afore-referred tyrannical poets came to be written and, what's worse, read. Poetry was the multiversal megastar; prose began its humble career as a dubious philological commentator. Betrayal and backstabbing belonged to another day, close at hand but hidden away. Centuries later, dedestructionists would study this phenomenon and tweet their findings – Poetry: fucked up by flattery and falsehood; Prose: proved talk is not cheap, turned purple, never got rid of its inclination to comment.

Back to this novel: Tamil in taste, English on the tongue, free of all poetry and prosody, dished out in dandy prose. Forgive this text its nagging tendency to try and explain, its disposition to tag its opinion at every turn of phrase. Please understand that staying verbose is a part of the process of prose. And also, please kindly understand that such underselling is clear evidence of my commitment to a supreme mission of self-sabotage.

Now, allow me an auspicious start. *Amen* and *Bismillah ir-Rahman ir-Rahim*. And so on and so forth. And, six times for the sacred sake of my mother-sexed tongue, *Murugamurugamurugamurugamurugamuruga.*

Once upon a time, in one tiny village, there lived an old woman.

Writing in the summer of the Spring Revolution, I anticipate everybody would be let down by an opening line that does not contain one oblique reference to a grenade, or a crusade, or even the underplayed and taboofied favourite, genocide. Homemade as slave trade and clichéd as conveyed, this beginning is meant to disappoint and devalue the great importance placed on grand entrances.

A first-generation woman novelist evidently working in a second language from that third-world country, literary critics may pooh-pooh and pin me down with prize-orange tartness after reading such a tame line, and prepare to expect nothing more than a domestic dramatic-traumatic tale. Let them jest in peace.

*

Once upon a time, in another tiny village, there lived another old woman.

This transplantation falls flat on its face, the fatal forehead first. Such a strategic shift of location and the introduction of a new population seem to have no effect on anybody's perception of a story. My Facebook fans, who have flocked around me in eager expectation of the clinching first line, have already deserted me. My family seems ready to disown me, friends prepare to fly away, and former lovers disappear. It dawns on me that readers have no patience for over-familiar tales or shared experiences. And how can I go ahead with the story when the first line itself has not instantly received a hundred thousand Likes?

Most people are tired of history, and also tired of history repeating itself, so I am constrained to try a new way to chart and plot my way past their boredom. Since fiction is all about reaching out to an anonymous audience, I shall try and drown my story in non-specificities for the first thousand and eight narrations.

*

Once upon some time, in some village of some size, there lived an old woman.

English, with its expertise of having administered the world, requires more efficiency. Not these breaks and starts. Perhaps the first line should frame the conflict and grip the reader with the revelation that this old woman eventually loses her extended family during a massacre. Or perhaps the first line should not bother about one old woman and, instead, it should reflect on a universal issue: untouchability or class struggle. Or perhaps the first line should not concern itself with character or conflict, and instead talk about the land that fed the world but forgot to feed all of her own people.

From what I have heard, place is always a good place to start. Nagapattinam, the theatre of the Old Woman's teary, fiery story. Tharangambadi, the village of her birth, land of the singing waves. Kilvenmani, the village into which she married, the village that married itself to communism. To handle that kind of overloaded opener, I need to dig up a lot of history.

*

It is common knowledge that no land would ever be found interesting until a white man arrived, befriended some locals, tried the regional cuisine, asked a lot of impertinent questions, took copious notes in his Moleskine notebook and then went back home and wrote something about it.

Ptolemy – part ethnic Greek, part Hellenized Egyptian – like other white men of dubious descent, took great pride in his knowledge of far-flung places and, succumbing to the pressures of the publication industry and his own mounting bills, set out to write a Lonely Planet guidebook, in which he made a passing, one-off reference to a Tamil port-city called Nigamos. Hurtled into history in this desperate fashion, Nagapattinam would patiently wait until a Tamil woman came along and decided to write a half-decent novel set in its surroundings.

Between the sixteenth and the twentieth centuries, Nagapattinam went from the very white hands of the Portuguese to the Dutch to the British. Even as she dallied with any of these varieties and every other walk-in *vellaikkaaran*, she kept intact her liaisons with the Arabs and the Chinese. Everyone stole her rice, and left religion as a souvenir. She lived with their gods, like old women often do. And because she managed to sink into their stories and make them her own, she rose above the other towns, metamorphosing from a sleepy port into a self-contained pilgrimage circuit.

In this land abounding in legends, one temple promises that God will be the Ender of Death; at Sikkal, Murugan receives the spear from his mother before he sets out to battle oppressive demons; bathing at a temple pond in Thirunallaru saves anybody from Saturn's seven-and-a-half-year itch. Religion reverses its role of divisive troublemaker: everybody flocks to the Nagore Sufi dargah; everybody with a desperate prayer walks on their knees to Our Lady of Velankanni. There is no accounting for taste, either: here, the usually bloodthirsty Kali is sated with *sakkarai pongal*, a sweet feast of rice cooked in jaggery, while the locals, a little distance away, will show you the exact place where the Buddha came with his lamp and sat under a tree and disappeared. Even St Anthony, who specializes in finding lost objects, came floating into their midst during a flood. Famed for its large chariot and its buxom devadasis, the temple at Tiruvarur once ensured that both gods and men were assured of a good ride. Then there's the temple for the pubescent Neelayadakshi, the only Tamil goddess with blue eyes. Clearly, some in the steady stream of visiting white men had spilled their seed.

*

Reverend Baierlein, translated from the German by a certain J. R. B. Gribble, observed in his book that the Danes docked at Nagapattinam, travelled north to Tharangambadi, the village where the Old Woman would one day be born, promptly named it Tranquebar, and set about preaching the purest gospel in place of all the gossip that was in circulation. This divinely preordained Danish coming involved the story of a shipwreck, an encounter with the king, and other recognizable features of Hollywood drama but, for a brief while, there was difficulty in casting the sacrificial heroes. While merchants and sailors from Denmark travelled here for trade – and the Tamil women's trusting eyes – no clergyman was man enough to take the Protestant missionary position in a strange, heathen land. Two Germans were dispatched instead, empty-handed, as the God and his son had asked them to go. With no recourse to evangelical funds, or medical insurance, Heinrich Plutschau stuck to the formula and proselytized without any fanfare and, after five years of puttering around, returned to Europe to defend the mission against critics.

But his companion, Bartholomaeus Ziegenbalg, began work zealously, rejecting both the Paulinian and Ottonian techniques of religious conversion, and formulating his own unique method for translating the word of God into heathen words. Not knowing the intricacies of what could be lost between slippery tongues, he learnt the local language by tracing the alphabet on a bed of sand, read all the 161 texts he could lay his hands on, sought a printing press (from the Danes, but the British supplied it), and placed orders for the Tamil typeface to be made in Halle. The type came, but it was too large and ate up all the paper, so he had the letters cut out of lead covers of Cheshire cheese tins, and went to work. Thus, he kept forcing himself on Mother Tamil, who, in order to guard her honour, put up a stiff fight against this alien seeking entry. But he kept at it, tested by the testaments and taunted by Tamil, and had just finished rendering the New Testament into this ruffian, rape-resisting tongue when the contemptuous Copenhagen clergy decided to summon him home again.

The German mangerman left for Madras – according to some reports, carried in a palanquin – in the hope that he might eventually be able to board a ship to Europe, and the people of his tiny congregation took his disappearance as a manifestation of divine wrath. They decided against disbanding (should Ziegenbalg return) and, to curry favour with their own briefly neglected pantheon, they resorted to the tried-and-tasted technique of sacrificing bellowing chickens and goats to their local, loudmouthed gods and goddesses.

*

Some poets are utter losers: unreliable when it comes to facts and incapable when it comes to fiction. Living in a territory that specialized in the development and deployment of torture devices to disfigure breasts, a lotus-eating bard deflected the demand for the appointment of a Special Rapporteur to the United Nations on this issue by playing with the people's imagination: he linked love to life and life to livelihood and livelihood to the land and the land to the local river and then, with a smiling simile he likened the lazy white river to a pearl necklace on the bosom of the earth, and in his picture-perfect poetry that sang of the River Cauvery, the bleeding, blinded breasts of slave labourers in this delta district were forgotten. I stand the risk of ridicule – it is true, the United Nations did not exist at that point in time, breasts are a beautiful metaphor any day, and one has to understand the importance of poetic licence. I am just spreading out the mattress on the riverside, setting up the landscape, inviting you, dear reader, to join me and look beyond the trauma, with the aid of such romantic imagery.

Kilvenmani, the village into which the Old Woman married, is irrigated by two tributaries of the Cauvery: Korai Aaru and Kaduvai Aaru. Korai, after the grass used to weave mats; Kaduvai, after a *Parai* drum special to the region. *Parai* as in *Paraiyar* as in the English 'pariah'. Rivers are to rice cultivation what lies are to poets: the lifeblood, some might say. Some life, some blood, I will hasten to add.

Initially, I wanted to put this section on poets and rivers down as a footnote and forget all about the fictional element. Last time I wrote a footnote, however, I made the mistake of suggesting that Ponnar and Sankar, two local guardian deities, were Arundhatiyars, an oppressed untouchable caste, and a case was slapped on me by the touchy touchable caste-Hindus seven years after the book appeared. I received a summons to court, and was charged with wantonly giving provocation with the intent to cause riot, and creating and promoting enmity, hatred and ill-will between different classes. So, my attempts to create a piece of fiction out of facts by telling a story from long, long ago, about an Old Woman in a tiny village, have been shelved until it is time for the thousand and ninth narration. Be consoled that to make up for the form being frivolous, the subject shall be serious.

*

Are you still hunting around for the one-line synopsis and the sixty-second sound bite? Do you want me to compress this tragedy to fit into Twitter? How does one even enter this heart of darkness?

Would you like to join Amy Goodman on *Democracy Now!* as she welcomes Krishnammal Jagannathan, the winner of an alternative Nobel Prize, a brave lady who espouses Gandhism and non-violence, who works to redistribute land to the tillers? Even as Goodman talks the old woman into revealing that she became an activist because of what happened at Kilvenmani, or that she cooked dosai for Martin Luther King during his India sojourn, watch for the bit where she gushes about the descendants of landlords coming in three cars and giving her all their title deeds. You can lean over and listen to them talk, but this sounds like a then-they-lived-happily-ever-after ending. It does not become a conflict-ridden start. Mere transcription is not an academically approved narrative style. Besides, the format of a video interview is a little too disciplined for a novel. This old woman is not the Old Woman of This Novel anyway.

Since it did not work out with Amy Goodman, can we go in search of another white woman to tell this story? There's Kathleen Gough, Left-leaning professor on the FBI's Watch List, who occasionally toured Tanjore district for her field trips. Women in Nagapattinam were known to have walked two or three villages to ask her one of two questions: whether white women menstruated, and whether they bathed their newborns in whisky to make them white. Popularity among the local population is an added bonus, but what's pertinent to this novel is the fact that she came here fifteen years before the tragedy. She also revisited eight years after. Years before I was born, she met some of the eyewitnesses I have met. Even her field notes from 1968 are still intact. If only I could get all of you to read her work, familiarize yourself with Marxist theory and take in all the information tucked away in the footnotes, I would have no need to write this novel. Sadly, you are too lazy for research papers.

To strike a fair balance, would you like to look into old American newspapers? Some headlines say the whole story: *Madras Is Reaping a Bitter Harvest of Rural Terrorism; Rice Growers' Feud With Field Workers Has Fiery Climax As Labor Seeks Bigger Share of Gain From Crop Innovations.*

In a way, that is all there is to it. This novel has only to fill in the blanks.

*

Should we go to the tiny village to learn its story? Or, should we stay here and continue studying history instead?

Can we use a big word that will rock the boat? *Slavery.* It feeds White guilt and it deprives Brown folk of a golden opportunity to take pride in being treated better than

Blacks. Disciplined novels are dead, well-behaved ones are damned, so allow me the opportunity to bring up this subject matter with a posh euphemism: emigration. In twelfth-century Tanjore, a slave could quote a price and sell himself. This practice did not fall into disuse – when the *vellaikkaaran* started coming, it evolved into a bazaar of manual labour. Like the dead disappearing into their graves, men going to the Coolie Export Depot at the Nagapattinam port were seldom seen again. If the landlords' men didn't manage to find the runaways at the harbour and drag them back to the fields, the coolies – they had become the word for their wage – ended up in Siam or Singapore or the Straits settlements as indentured labourers, becoming bonded to British plantations and railroad projects. Tens of thousands died working but timid readers will not survive that history, so let us stick to the theme that concerns our novel.

But, before that, a brief interlude anyway: would they have lived if they had stayed? In 1646, on a Portuguese vessel that came to Sumatra via our Nagapattinam, there were 400 hunger-starved slaves who couldn't lift a limb. Sold half-price when they were brought ashore, they spoke of the famine in their land that had swallowed their old ones, their young ones and their talkative ones. Four hundred years later, famine and feudal torture keep throwing them about and, in fear, they keep taking flight.

(The more things change, the more they remain the same. Never mind.)

Many of these Tamil 'emigrants' ended up in Malaya, where they found themselves in every trade union of mine workers and dock workers and ferry workers. Then the government started swatting Communists like mosquitoes and some outspoken Tamil workers were charged with treason, their leader Comrade Ganapati was hanged, and even engaging Lee Kwan Yew as their legal adviser to fight the deportation case did not help matters. Comrade Veerasenan was shot on the high seas off Singapore and only a few men from Malaya – Senan, Iraniyan, and others – managed to get back to India and smuggle communism into their motherland. Labour export, communism import – it is too early to fetishize a foreign commodity that springs out of slave trade. Stay silent and perfect your solemnity. Let me search for its local roots.

*

Anyone could, at some point, object to this narrative because it alternates between leading the characters and leading the audience. The story, working hard to break the stranglehold of narrative, does not dabble in anything beyond agriculture. All of fiction's artefacts used in this novel – lining, holing, filling, mixing, planting, staking, topping, weeding, watering, manuring, threshing, winnowing – are borrowed from a peasant's paradise. Here, stories grow like haphazard weeds. Here, ideas flow like rain through leaky thatched roofs.

Thread One: communism thrived in East Tanjore because this place had the highest number of discussion-inducing tea stalls in the province. It was often suggested, by none other than the decaffeinated bourgeoisie, that communism would be eradicated if tea ceased to exist. *Thread Two:* communism crept up only along the railway lines. *Thread Two Point Two One:* twentieth-century Marxists would turn feudal, almost fascist, and seek to silence everybody who spoke of caste in place of class. *Thread Two Point Four:* the first posters of Chairman Mao began to appear towards the end of 1968. Sometimes, Comrade Ho Chi Minh put in a special graffiti appearance. *Thread Three:* a young man (native informant, with the added bonus of being the author's father) shudders first, then celebrates, on hearing the story of a class enemy (a landlord of Irinjiyur) being axed into four and forty pieces, his dead flesh wrapped in palm fronds and given away to peasant families as a souvenir of revenge. *Thread Five:* the first Communist protest in Tanjore seeking higher wages in agriculture takes place in 1943. *Thread Six:* if the people were to sight a Communist in hiding, they were to ring the temple bells in order to alert the police. *Thread Seven:* close to a thousand Naxalite Communists on remand are brought to Tamil

Nadu because the prisons in West Bengal do not have the capacity to hold them all. *Thread Eleven:* every owner of a gun or revolver or pistol, or any other fire-arm, should deposit the weapon (with ammunition) at the local police station, obtain the safe-custody receipt, fill out a renewal form and wait until procedural formalities are finished over the course of a week. This bureaucratic procedure ensured that even the most trigger-happy landlords were left unarmed for a period of time. The militant Naxalites, with their liquidation-of-landlords programme, waited for ages for the arrival of this week of disarmament. *Thread Thirteen:* mobilization of the agricultural slaves by the Communists put an end to inhuman feudal practices.

Rest assured, dear reader: you are intelligent enough to find all the missing threads and tie up the loose ends. People in this land predict rain from the sound of faraway thunder, patterns of the dragonfly in flight, halos around the moon, answers of the spirit-possessed dancers, the probability of picking vermilion over sacred ash and other random occurrences. Have hope, my fiction is much more fixed.

*

Just because this is a novel set in rural India, do not expect a herd of buffalo to walk across every page for the sake of authenticity. Eager mothers who hold salt and dried red chillies and circle their hands over your head before asking you to spit into their palms three times to trick spirits of the evil eye into abandoning you have been held back at my behest because I do not want to lose you to nostalgia or exotica. The tinkling bells of bullocks could add music to these sentences, but they have been muted so that you can silently stalk the storyline.

Comrade, let's get this clear. There are only two possible ways of going about this. If you were able to get your papers stamped in the right places, if you have purchased your tickets, I could take you to the village of Kilvenmani and let you immerse yourself in the lifestyle there. I could let you live with them through the seasons, teach you to whistle as you work alongside them in the rice fields in a half-hearted attempt to declass yourself, hold your hand as you watch the sunset and call it spectacular every single time, let you walk back home with my women. I could teach you what it means to winnow when the wind blows, how to sweep up the leftover grain on a threshing floor, how much the various measures hold, and how to walk with a bundle of firewood on your head. I could cook you gruel and watch you greedily relish it with raw onion. I could show you the sculpted shoulders of the working men; I could make you swoon at the sight of their sweat. I could make you listen to a grandmother's curse, a mother's lullabies, an aunt's dirges. I could ask the roving gypsy woman to tattoo your arms and your legs with an ink made from mothers' milk. I could provide you the pleasure of being an economy-class voyeur on this exotic time-travel. And this would continue ad nauseam and you would be sick of the cloying sweetness. And chances are, you would never learn.

The only other way of doing this is the way I am doing it.

*

The gods in these lands outnumber the people. The demons in these lands outperform Satan. The devils are whirlwinds during daylight; they toss every twig and trembling leaf that comes their way. At night they assume other lives – turning into flickering lights, or stealthy, lamp-eyed cats or a corpse-lady walking backwards. They compete in cross-country racing in the dark, riding on invisible horses. Some demons are held responsible for failure in trade, most of them specialize in ruining crops. At some point of time in their lives, most demons are said to have taken part in stone-throwing and vandalizing public property. On drunken nights, they have caused whole villages to be deserted. If the Old Woman were to be believed, the primary agenda of these demons is to cause terror, and the most malicious of them have been known to set fire to thatched roofs. Watch out for these terrorizing demons, going about setting fire to thatched roofs.

Like the lone monkey in a coconut tree that has nothing better to do than mock itself, I perform these narrative gimmicks to amuse myself. Much later, like the monkey, I might get a decent audience; I might even do these tricks for a living. I could launch into an enumerative, explanatory list of the tricks employed to tell any story in the magic realism mode. I desist because it is an unfair playing field. I am in no mood to give the game away. So, let us trot back to realism. There is Maayi the Old Woman. There is Muniyan the Village Headman. There is Gopalakrishna Naidu the Landlord. There is Muthusamy the Communist. There is Sikkal Pakkirisamy the Slain.

Keep in mind, though, that this narrator-novelist draws inspiration from Tamil mystics – shrinking to a microscopic speck, burgeoning into a ten-headed demon, assuming weightlessness, turning leaden, taking flights of fancy, transmigrating into other bodies, assuming authority and charming everybody. This fatal flaw in her prose follows her faithfully.

*

Do you suspect a murder merely because of this fancy prose style? Do you want a puppet-show in place of all this meandering prose? Do you rue the fact that modernism and postmodernism have killed our storytelling traditions? I am willing to try everything to get this story across. So, here I am, pitching a tent under a tree, propping up a blank screen, pulling out my puppets. Come, take a peek. Authority is easy to caricature. The puppets with the overgrown handlebar moustaches are landlords. The puppets with a stoop worked into their backs and a squeal stamped into their voices are the landless. The stiff-necked puppets who march as a pack are the policemen. And the mysterious Old Woman: she's the puppet with a head that shakes during the storytelling. She's the puppet who beats her sagging breasts to mourn, to make a point, to curse, to cry a call to arms. You do not see her face, the fading brown of her eyes, the skin collapsing into wrinkles. You do not get that close to the storyteller. The play of light here works with a binary logic – bright lamps cast dark shadows. And the shadows tell their stories as you watch them move and mimic the voices of men and women and birds and animals. Squatting, arms around your knees, wide-eyed, open-mouthed, you take away the story as the puppets walk the talk. When they are done, most puppets disappear. Some stay. Some drop dead.

If you are the emotional type, the puppet-show is not any easier than this book.

*

How does this work of art seek to declare itself?

It plagiarizes the most scathing criticism, it prides itself on its ability to disappoint. Why bother about the pain of accomplishing something and arriving somewhere, when failure has been made a flashy trophy in itself? Humility is a convoluted highlight. Even this book's obituary is a copy; it steals verbatim from someone else's words to describe its own shortcomings; it keeps the reproduced text from all knowledge of the original – assuming that never the Twain shall meet; and thus, the borrowed barbs glow like a golden back-cover blurb:

'It has no invention; it has no order, system, sequence, or result; it has no lifelikeness, no thrill, no stir, no seeming of reality; its characters are confusedly drawn, and by their acts and words they prove that they are not the sort of people the author claims that they are; its humor is pathetic; its pathos is funny; its conversations are – oh! indescribable; its love-scenes odious; its English a crime against the language.'

For the sake of clarification, its English is *Taminglish.*

Everything is so precariously held together here that you might want a helping hand. Nobody is going to teach you that right after a harvest, poorly paid labourers were hungry enough to smoke out rodent holes and steal back the grains of paddy pilfered by rats. But you will manage. You will learn to relate without family trees. You will learn to make do without a village map. You will learn that criminal landlords can break civil laws to enforce caste codes. You will learn that handfuls of rice can consume half a village. You will later learn that in the eyes of the law, the rich are incapable of soiling their hands with either mud or blood. You will learn to wait for revenge with the patience of a village awaiting rain.

If you are finding this difficult to follow, remember that not only am I weighed down by the task of telling a story, but also that you are equally responsible for your misery. Art depicts people. So, this degenerate narrative merely mirrors the fact that all of you, my darling readers, have been living non-linear, amoral lives without any sense of purpose. Life is linear, I can hear you argue. It is, but it is cyclical, too. If you ask a mathematician, she will tell you that life possibly exists in the *n*th dimension, and beyond the third, none of your fucking senses can perceive anything at all. That's where stories unravel themselves. Those of you stressed out by this haphazard storytelling, please relax. Stay, those of you who have thought too many times of wandering away. How far away from me can you stray? This is a joint venture. We collaborate on the critical condition that we do not abandon each other.

*

Abandoning is old hat in literature, so this cry for commitment stems from insecurity.

I have been dabbling in the art of abandoning, too. Once, being impressed with the French Anarchist writer Félix Fénéon and his *Novels in Three Lines*, I attempted to adapt his brilliant, fragmented form to continue to tell my version of the story of the Old Woman in a tiny village. Over the course of considerable time, I was able to write a few tiny excerpts of her history, but I gave up, unable to sustain my momentum. The entire story that I was waiting to tell seemed to lie outside her. Did she have it in her to hold a village together? Could I show everything in these snippets? Riddled with self-doubt, I stopped trying to make my story fit into this form.

It was an interesting experiment while it lasted. Weeks later, I felt my jottings were not good enough to get into the book because the characters had not got into them. Once I realized that becoming a mistress of the compress-and-express form of storytelling was not for me, I played with the idea of moving on. Out of habit, I lingered, toying with these time-release capsules:

> One Karuppaayi of Thiruchuli village in the Ramnad district recounts that, during the great famine, she lost her husband and her three little sons. She managed to stay alive eating handfuls of mud. Taking pity on her because of her pregnant condition, a relief worker fed her congee every day.

> In December 1877, the Gundar River in Ramnad swelled suddenly, breaking her banks in her haste to meet the sea. Karuppaayi went to Tranquebar, finding shelter at the home

of the relief worker who saved her life. Many others were not as lucky – they survived the famine but not the floods; the *Royal Gazetteer* recorded over a thousand deaths in the first week.

Chinnamma of Irukkai died on 15 August 1925 from complications arising out of childbirth. The death, due to septic shock, resulted from the use of an agricultural sickle to cut her umbilical cord. The newborn was handed over to her grandmother, Karuppaayi, a domestic help of Europeans in Tranquebar.

Tranquebar is reeling from the shock of witnessing the sixtieth rape of the last three weeks. Dragged from her grandmother's home at the outskirts of the town, the fourteen-year-old girl heard nothing but her own screams through the night; the landlord-rapists did not stop, nor did they dignify her with a single word. Sources in Nagapattinam confirm that no case was filed.

(Preliminary reports indicate the rape took place on the night of 16 December 1939. The gang-rape victim's name has been withheld for reasons of anonymity. She will be referred to as 'She' in all reports, including in the regular, feel-good stories that we are committed to publishing.)

She went to Sannasi, a wandering witch doctor, the strongest man She saw. Sannasi's priesthood ended when She offered him the wondrous pleasure of her breasts. Before the next summer, they were married and She had given birth to his son.

When the exiled Thayyan, the witch doctor's brother, was found to have crept back to Kilvenmani to steal a look at his one-year-old nephew, he was beaten to death, doused in kerosene and set alight. For concealing information about their brother's visit, Sannasi and Periyaan were whipped mercilessly. Police declared Thayyan's death as an arson-related accident on the landlord Porayar's farm.

On 14 April 1965, untouchables around Keevalur dismantled a temple chariot in protest at not being granted the right to pull it through the streets. Caste-Hindus retaliated by burning the 'defiled' chariot. Sannasi, suspected mastermind of this protest, was abducted the next day, and his body turned up two weeks later in Karaikkal. Police have closed the case as a mysterious death.

To avenge her husband's death, Sannasi's widow stepped out on the Communist Party circuit. Asked to describe her, a comrade in Kilvenmani said, 'She knows what to say when, how to say what, when to start a why, where to cease the talk.' Similarly pressed, a landlord said, 'Oh! The Old Woman? That troublemaking Communist cunt? That untouchable whore? Get out of here.'

This time, I moved on.

*

Finally, if you want the phony and the polyphony, the hysterical and the polyhistorical, wait for the postcolonial version, where the dusky Old Woman of my story takes after the pale Janie of Zora Neale Hurston's. They are both women who believe that the dream is the truth. They are both widowed women who learn to press their teeth together, who learn to hush. They are both women who find their wisdom poses a great challenge to others because, sometimes, God gets familiar with them and tells them secrets about men. They are both women full of life.

They are both women who think alike of Death as that strange being with the huge square toes who lives in the straight house like a platform without sides or a roof and who stands watchful and motionless all day with his sword drawn back, waiting for a messenger to bid him come, and who has been standing there before there was a where or a when or a then. They are both women who have come back from burying the dead.

Not just the dead, but the sudden dead.

*

Enough about the Old Woman. You will soon get to hear her speak, watch her move.

Meanwhile, remember this: nobody lived happily. Nobody outlived the ever-after.

2. *The Title Misdeed*

When you are high on caffeine and contemporary authors, you begin to question the fundamentals of the publishing industry, which you think owes it to you to make your novel widely read. After all, for the sake of reading widely, you have contributed an unfortunately large amount of your small income to the said industry.

Take the title for instance: it has to be catchy, it has to incite curiosity, it has to sound cool when you say it to others. That's why I settled on this one. Well, almost. It satisfies all of the above criteria.

The minute you realize that the novel is quite unlike the university dissertation, you gain the necessary courage to be experimental. You will soon realize, especially if you have been confounded by Derrida-Schmerrida at college, that a book does not have to be about its title. A title does not have to be about the book. Trust me, they are generous enough to co-exist with each other.

If you ask me upfront, I will tell you that this novel has

nothing to do with the title. You are not my agent, anyway. A nice title would have been *Long Live Revolution!* Or, *The Red Flag*. Or, as Žižek once said, when asked to share a secret with the *Guardian* during an interview, *Communism Will Win*. Sadly, the Communists will be outraged to be glorified in such an archetypal bourgeois literary form such as the novel, which they will contend has been produced for the global market. The other trouble with these titles is that it could get my novel into serious, life-threatening situations. Customs officials in a few faraway lands could hammer spikes through it or it could be pulped by a paper-shredder in quasi-repressive states. My books of poetry have been burnt. This novel is a delicate darling, and I will not let this happen to her. She has to live. She has to be in love. She has to see the world. For all that, she has to be named.

In the beginning, I did not want to cheat. I thought of good titles. *Tales from Tanjore* had an authentic ring to it, but those who picked up such a book would end up disappointed when they did not come across tigers, Tipu Sultan and the Pudukkottai royalty. Then again, *Butcher Boys* had the sound of a college music band, and little relevance to this novel except reflecting some of the bloodthirsty rage that romps around in these pages. *Kilvenmani* gave away the location, and a friend said it had a distinct Irish ring to it, so I dropped it as a gesture of goodwill because

I didn't want to mislead my readers. In a similar manner, *Christmas Day* gave away the date, but that title would make the reader imagine snow and reindeers and pine trees, and the entire seasonal marketing mania, instead of imagining peasant agitations. It would be the equivalent of using the word 'holocaust' somewhere in the title, only because you wanted to refer to a massacre where sacrificial victims were completely burnt to death. (Christmas Day, did I say? In *Jailbird*, Kurt Vonnegut wrote of the fictional Cuyahoga massacre that involved industrial action and took place on 25 December. The problem with thinking up a new and original idea within a novel is that you have to make sure that Kurt Vonnegut has not already thought of it.) So, I gave up on that title and, for some time, I wanted to name it *1968*, the most tumultuous year of recent history, the year in which the central incident of this novel occurs. But Orwell has been there before me with this year-as-title thingy. What's more painful is that he used my year of birth without my explicit consent.

There go all my titles, and any effort at sincerity. Now I am out of choices. So I settle on the curiously obscure and mildly enchanting choice, *The Gypsy Goddess*.

I have a great title. I have a great story.

They don't belong to each other. In this author-arranged marriage-without-divorce, these two will stay together.

Considering the title of this chapter, I should technically

have completed one obligation: unravel the mystery of the title. So, here is the abridged version of the legend of the Gypsy Goddess. Go ahead, read it. These are two minutes of your life that you are never getting back.

This story begins with an epic novelist, who, having penned a racy thriller involving a hetero-normative love pentagon between three men and two women, enjoys enormous popularity and unparalleled critical, commercial and cultural success. At the zenith of his glory, he realizes that his characters have outgrown his epic and have become household names. Every day, he hears of fanclubs being started for his hero, beauty parlours and massage centres named after his heroine, and body-building gyms being inaugurated in the name of the hero's side-kick brother. And, much as his characters inspire love, they also inspire hate. He witnesses the effigy of his villain being burnt at street corners across the country. He hears stories of men, reeling under the influence of his epic heroes, cutting off the noses of women who have lust in their eyes. This horror, this horror is too much to take. His greatest creation, his labour of love, has turned into a nation's Frankenstein's monster. He foresees a future of massacre and mayhem, bloodshed and bomb-blasts, deaths and demolition.

So he fled to foreign shores.

He travelled far and wide and here and there in search of anonymity and, finally, he decided to settle down in a

Tamil village where the men had as many gods as their forefathers had found the leisure to invent, where the business of customized, cash-on-delivery idol-making flourished and kept up with the demands of the idol-worshippers, where the men and the women and the children called upon their lord gods every time they had a nervous tic or whooping cough or a full bladder or a mosquito bite or a peg of palm toddy or an argument with the local thug, where they boozed and banged around every day of every week, where they affectionately addressed their fathers as mother-fuckers, where they killed and committed adultery and stole and lied about everything at the court and the confession box, where they coveted each other's concubines and wives, and where they did all of this because the script demanded it. Evidently, this village in Tanjore was an author's paradise.

They welcomed him with proverbial open arms. Being unrepentant idol-worshippers, they soon cast the charismatic novelist into the role of a demigod and rechristened him Mayavan, Man of Illusion & Mystery. He was consulted on every important decision regarding the village community. In perfect role-reversal, they told him stories.

The exile ignored their stories for days on end, not allowing any character to have the slightest impact on him out of fear that he would slip into writing once again. But, as was bound to happen, one story about Kuravars, the roaming nomad gypsies, caught his fancy, drove him into a frenzy and rendered him sleepless.

On one night, many many nights ago, seven gypsy women, carrying their babies, strayed and lost their way whilst walking back to their camp. When they came home the next day, the seven women were murdered along with their babies. Their collective pleading did not help. Some versions go on to add that there were seventeen women. Every version agrees that all of them had children with them. Some versions say these women and their children were forced to drink poison. Some versions say that these women were locked in a tiny hut and burnt to death along with their children. Some gruesome versions say that these women were ordered to run and they had their heads chopped off with flying discs and their children died of fright at seeing their mothers' beheaded torsos run. It is said that after these murders, women never stepped out of the shadows of their husbands.

The novelist, ill at ease, wants to teach a lesson to the village. In one stroke, he elevates the seven condemned women and their children into one cult goddess. He divines that unless these dead women are worshipped, the village shall suffer ceaselessly.

Overnight, the villagers build a statue of mud of Kurathi Amman, the Gypsy Goddess, and say their first prayers. Misers come to ruin, thieves are struck blind, wife-beaters sprout horns, rapists are mysteriously castrated, and murderers are found dead the following morning, their bodies mutilated beyond recognition.

Faith follows her ferocity. Over time, she becomes the reigning goddess.

She loves an animal slaughtered in her honour every once in a while but, mostly, she is content with the six measures of paddy that are paid to her on every important occasion.

Full disclosure: for all my irreligiosity, Kurathi Amman is rumoured to be my ancestral goddess. And Mayavan is the ancestral deity of a man I once loved. Our deities live the happily-ever-after fairy tale while we drift around with poetry and politics to numb and dissolve our pain.

Sad story, indeed.

Now, you can forget all about this and move on to the novel.

Fuck these postmodern writers.

part two

BREEDING GROUND

* * *

3. *The Cutthroat Comrades*

Gopalakrishna Naidu had inherited all of Gandhi's adamancy, most of his self-righteousness and a wee bit of his desire to save humanity. Upon realizing that he was endowed with such a desirable mix of messianic attributes, he fashioned himself as a father-figure for the landlords of Nagapattinam and, therefore, took upon himself the timeless task of protecting their vested and invested interests. As required of self-made heroes who shoulder such responsibility, he satisfied all the requisite criteria: he perfected the role of a leader who represented hope, claimed to symbolize change even as he continued to believe in age-old values, and unfailingly met his constituency on a regular basis. Having introduced this balding, middle-aged man in three-and-a-half formidable sentences, I step aside as a big-mouthed narrator-novelist, and instead invite you to catch him on his campaign trail.

On a sultry afternoon in July, when the sun sets the sky on fire, Gopalakrishna Naidu's gleaming pleasure-car (simply called 'pleasure' by the villagers, and 'car' by those who have travelled in one) arrives at the doorstep of Ramu Thevar's palatial bungalow, having traversed a picturesque Tanjore countryside replete with lakes and rivers and lush-green rice fields and tropical coconut trees. In a cinematic wide-angle shot, the door of the ash-coloured Ambassador opens and we first spot Gopalakrishna Naidu's gold-ringed right hand, and then we see the rest of him emerge, dressed in spotless hand-spun, hassle-free white cotton. As you visualize him walking from his car to his designated place, here's the background song that should fill your eager ears: *one in a million million/ he walks like a kingly lion/ one in a million million/ he wears red red vermillion/ one in a million million/ he's here to crush the rebellion.* Trust me, such music sounds really upbeat when rapped in Tamil; what you see here is the tragedy of translation while the central character makes a transition.

Seated, saluted, and having sipped the customary filter coffee, he begins business without further ado. Out of a compelling need to hear his own voice, and also because of the curiosity of the other landlords to learn the precise tenor of a bachelor baritone which commands and controls the entire district, Gopalakrishna Naidu is the first to address the Emergency Executive Committee Meeting of the Paddy Producers Association. Reality competes with cinematic representation when he takes control of the floor: his audience looks keen; his speech stings; and his body, anaesthetized by this power-trip, appears motionless below the shoulders. He begins a rapid-fire round of attack.

Govinda Raja Naidu, next-door neighbour and distant cousin, is handpicked to be the first sacrificial victim. 'Our Kerosene Govinda has done us proud. Why do you think we are having this emergency meeting today? To celebrate his achievement. To congratulate this braveheart. His name now resonates in all eight directions. Soon, his face will become very familiar throughout the district when the Communists start putting up posters. Who knows, he may show up on the cinema posters, too. After all, more people watched our hero charging through Thevur market shouting death threats than watched MGR in *Nadodi Mannan*.'

Some landlords laugh nervously. Gopalakrishna Naidu goes on. 'Brother, carelessness will catch up with you soon. You will be dead meat before the word "kerosene" in your name has dried up. Indifference will not help. Every time a Communist corpse turns up, our peace is lost. The police hound us like dogs. If their local leaders, Thevur Kannan or Sikkal Pakkirisamy, hang themselves, or even if they hang each other, the Communists will blame us. Cases would be filed against us. If something happens to those dogs now, six villages will rush to the witness box. Will you then summon ghosts to give evidence in your favour? I do not ask any of you to be afraid of the cutthroat comrades. There is no other man in East Tanjore who has earned their hatred as much as me. I am their enemy number one. They have turned our own people against us, so we should know when to be daring and when to be discreet.'

At this point, it suddenly strikes me that every authoritative villain must stroke something and keep his hands busy. Like Vito Corleone and Blofeld with cats. Sadly, Gopalakrishna Naidu is a dog person. Moreover, Tommy, his Alsatian, has never been allowed to climb on to his lap. So I dismiss this stray idea, abandon my quest for a prop, and return to the story. A few things have transpired since we drifted off, but I don't think we have missed much.

'There is no need to introduce the next hero in our midst. His lands are spread across eight villages but, being wrapped up in his manly exploits, this *minor* finds no time to attend to agriculture, or our useless association.'

The second target is Ramanuja Naidu. Gopalakrishna Naidu has quickly battered the fragile egos of some of his relatives and so he finds himself on a moral high-ground. Whom does he pick next? Not Balakrishna Naidu, his nephew. Not Murthy, his agent who is seated to his right. Not Damu. Not Kittu. Not Perumal Naidu. Not Narayanasamy Pillai. Not Kothandam Pillai. Not any puppet. Not Pakkirisami Pillai of Irukkai, lifeline for imported labour. Not the Porayar father–son duo, landlords living in Kilvenmani (according to information circulated by the Communists, the father was a routine pimp). Not Andhakkudi Chinnaswamy Iyer, famous in the district for throwing stones at untouchables who entered his street. Not Adikesavalu. Not any of the other henchmen. Not Arumuga Mudaliar, his old enemy. Not Ramu Thevar, the treasurer. Not even the loud-mouthed Sambandhamoorthy Mudaliar, or his agent Kaathaan Perumal. Not Kayarohanam Chettiar, *mirasdar* moneylender of Nagapattinam. Each of them will have to wait for their turn.

'People say that you joined the Communists. I hope it is only gossip.' He singles out Ganapati Nadar. 'But who can stop these ignorant people from speaking whatever comes into their minds? And they have good reason to say what they are saying. Every village in Nagapattinam sports our association flag, doesn't it? Except the village of Kilvenmani, which has the fortune of being owned by you, and the misfortune of being covered in red flags. Forgive me, Comrade Ganapati, if your stomach churns at all this talk but, seriously, are you thinking of upstaging us?'

Ramu Thevar attempts to intercede, but agent Murthy silences him with his eyes. As Gopalakrishna Naidu's Man Friday, this is an official obligation.

Shocked into standing, his body considerably stooped, Ganapati hastily professes his loyalty and his devotion.

'I have asked them to remove the red flags – even yesterday I did – many times I did.'

'Oh! You want me, you want us, to believe you. All the red cloth in Nagapattinam flies in that village. But how would you have seen it? Both your wives have kept you busy.'

Ganapati Nadar is taken aback by this abrupt attack, but he remains silent. Meanwhile, established as a villain within these first few pages, and resembling a no-nonsense man because of all the fictional fleshing out, Gopalakrishna Naidu takes the initiative to work on his dialogue delivery.

'You can ask them again and again. It is better if you make them mend their ways. Otherwise I will have to intervene and teach a lesson to every Pallan and Paraiyan and Chakkili. Everybody knows what happened to untouchables in my village – Irinjiyur is communism-free. If they want to stay on our land, they should obey our rules. If they do not want to obey us, they can remain underground for ever, like their comrade Chinnapillai. They can continue being Communist without causing trouble to others.

'Your problem is that you stop at asking them. They are not obedient, they do not listen to you. They talk back to you, for you have pampered them. This cannot go on for long. You go back to them and deal with them in the manner in which they should be dealt with. Or you can join them, and I can deal with all of you.

'Look, tell me the name of the troublemakers. We will

take them one by one. Dead people do not speak or shout in public meetings. They are silent and well behaved, and they serve as a good example to others.'

There is a long, drawn-out, dramatic silence. Ukkadai Muthukrishna Naidu, the other *mirasdar* in Kilvenmani, enthusiastically agrees, glad that Ganapati Nadar is taking the rap. The encouragement makes Gopalakrishna Naidu even more garrulous.

'Let the Communists know that we will never succumb to their blackmail tactics. They take their processions through our streets, they hold meetings in our grounds. The threat of violence is out in the open: it is in their songs, it is in their slogans. Should we let ourselves be terrorized in this manner? Is it not our duty to tell the people about the true colours of the Communists? Because we have a few thigh-twitching, weak-kneed landlords in our midst does not mean that we will be bamboozled by these outcastes. It is not enough if we strike a deal with some of their leaders and sit back silently. It is our personal responsibility to make sure that none of us is held hostage by them. We will do whatever it takes, but we will not concede to the demands of these coolies, or their leaders. Today you have all come running to me because they asked for an extra half measure of rice. If you give it today, they will ask for ten measures tomorrow. If you let them enter your home, they will want to sleep on your bed. Nothing we give them will be enough for them, so it is better that they are given nothing to begin with. Let them complain.'

Now, he looks around the room, at the nodding heads, and calls them out as if it were an award function: 'Kerosene Govinda, Balakrishna, Ramanuja, Murthy, Kittu – murder case. Kothandam, Porayar – rape case. Ramu Thevar – abduction and attempted murder case. Even Mudaliar ayya must have had complaints filed against him in his younger days. Vinayagam ayya is not here with us at the moment. He sent word that he shall come and visit me tomorrow. Can anybody even count the number of times he has been investigated? He was there in every movement, and now he is with the ruling party, he is, in fact, the biggest DMK politician in our area. He is a daring man, cases cannot shake him. One has to learn from him that a complaint against you means you are doing good work. A case means you are doing very good work.'

Everyone appears relieved. Intoxicated by an audience that admires every word he utters, Gopalakrishna says, 'Any case should not make us afraid. It is leadership quality. Today I have the highest number of complaints against me. Today, I scold Kerosene Govinda because he recklessly got into trouble. Tomorrow, I am the first man to help him. Why? Because I know about the Complaint Party. Police complaint, minister complaint, chief minister complaint. There is no limit.

'The Communists have sent sixteen petitions in the last three months. They have one department to write articles against the government, and they have another department to write memorandums to the government. I know that there are some full-timer thugs whose only job it is to write a police complaint on behalf of every Pallan and Paraiyan who walks into the party office. The English-educated lordships in our midst may fail to record the minutes of our meetings, but we should not forget that our moves are being faithfully filed away as complaints. Tomorrow, if they take away all our lands, make us beggars, throw us into prison, we cannot blame politics or policy. We have to blame our lack of paperwork.'

Srinivasa Naidu and Seshappa Iyer scribble furiously, with renewed vigour. Each of them wishes he could shift uneasily in his chair, making it easier for the reader to feel his state of discomfort but, unfortunately, this is a rural novel and it is considered a sign of insolence in Tamil culture to throw your weight around. So they sit still, and wait for the tirade to end.

He picks out his last targets.

'Look at these Brahmins in our midst. They run away at the sight of trouble. So many of them have moved out from their *agraharam* and fled to the cities. Street after exclusive street now lies deserted. They cannot face the enemy because they are too afraid. We are stronger, we are braver.

We have grown on meat, we are men. We don't have to end up in Delhi or Calcutta or London. We can stay and fight.'

At least three landlords in the room, who have been previously beaten up by him, can testify that this is Gopalakrishna Naidu at his genial best. The upbraiding and downgrading appears to have come to an end. Explanations are not sought. Or offered.

Devious like all diplomatic despots, and having injected the necessary dose of reverence, he now covers government-related safe ground: we have to oppose the new state-levied tax on irrigation because it is backbreaking to small farmers ('They tax land, they tax water, will the party of the rising sun next tax light?'); we have to demand an official quality-control flying squad as fertilizers do not live up to their promised potency ('These days, the companies spend more on advertising their products than on producing them'); we have to condemn the delay in plunging bore-wells in the district ('This is a government of gravediggers. They will get to work only when they see dead people').

Tough talk coupled with a liberal use of the royal plural elicits the right reaction: there is a discernible change of mood, and as tracking shots from our snack table reveal, other landlords (and their henchmen) are seen gazing in wide-eyed admiration, chuckling or looking dumbstruck at appropriate intervals, or nodding in emphatic agreement.

Now that he has successfully manufactured consent-based camaraderie, Gopalakrishna Naidu moves on to the next stage. To whip up anger, he steps up his multi-pronged attack on the inefficiency of the brainless and spineless government officials. The atmosphere created by the absence of the local DMK leader, Vinayagam Naidu, makes his task easier. 'How can the price of food grain alone be forced to remain static when fertilizer prices multiply every day? Why was the planning commission's recommendation to increase the price of paddy by fifty rupees for each quintal not implemented? If we have to go to court to restore every right, why does a Madras government exist? Why do these ministers dream of cultivating a million acres in the coming crop season, and, more importantly, where are these million acres? Are they not aware of the difficulties we face? Have they forgotten how the demon of communism has laid waste to our lands? Would they care if we went without food as long as we gave up all our grain for the civil supply? If Madras was plunged into darkness like Nagapattinam, and cursed with such sporadic electricity, would they be able to live a single day? Do they think of our people as prostitutes and pimps and petty thieves who need the blackness of night to commit crimes? Has their police force ever protected us? If any khaki-clad man had been born to one father, would not he rip out his tongue and die of shame, instead of smiling when the Communists shower abuses on the police in meeting after meeting? How can we expect protection from impotent men who cannot even protect themselves?'

You scoff at this speech and look at me as if I were his designated ghostwriter. You ask me if I made him rehearse this material with me for days. You point out that under normal circumstances, questions do not flow in such spontaneous succession.

I beg to disagree.

Now, how do I clear the air? Like all other writers before me, I ask you to trust me. Each mannerism of Gopalakrishna Naidu has been researched thoroughly and documented solely for the purpose of this novel – I could offer an accredited course about him if someone were willing to pay me to teach. In fact, this angry and ready-made rhetoric has enabled him to establish himself as a local leader. If you asked him (without sounding sarcastic or stupid) about his ability to breathlessly argue, he would be kind enough to admit that this is indeed a plus-point.

I hope this was convincing enough. Now, let me back into Ramu Thevar's living room so that I can continue reporting.

Gopalakrishna Naidu's barrage of questions is still being meticulously noted down by Seshappa Iyer, secretary of the Paddy Producers Association. Cunning by practice and advocate by profession, he will later convert every rhetorical rigmarole that Gopalakrishna Naidu spat out into statistically substantiated, pressingly urgent, gravely important, bullet-pointed legalese that will masquerade as a memorandum of demands submitted to the government. His experience in law, the English language, and pulling the right strings makes him indispensable to the Paddy Producers Association and Iyer, devoid of charm but aware of the influence he wields, is the only one to interrupt Gopalakrishna Naidu.

'One doesn't lick the back of his hand when he carries honey in his palm,' he says.

'We are not dogs to live by licking,' Gopalakrishna Naidu retorts, but picks up the proverbial cue.

Now he takes the help of a whore named History and, girding himself for action, rushes into flashback mode with a personal tragedy: his father died of disgrace when slogan-shouting agricultural labourers organized a demonstration waving slippers in the air. Unable to come to terms with his early, unexpected death (that factually took place 713 days after the provocative procession), his mother committed suicide (on her sixth and definitive attempt) by drinking the dust of her diamond nose-ring.

'We have made sacrifices in our struggle. We have been outnumbered by the Communists but we have managed to fight them. It is true that we have money, it is true that the politicians stand by us, but what we are doing is simply not enough. We do not know for how long this goodwill will last. Day by day, the Communists are growing stronger. For ten rupees at Chakravarti Press, they make a thousand copies of their handbills and posters and shame us everywhere. It is our duty to protect the public interest. We should prevent Communist propaganda from seeping into us, from dividing us from our own people. Do our coolies even stop to think that their huts stand on lands that we own? Do they consider it wrong when they stake claim over our lands without realizing that they are merely men who have come to work the paddy fields for a small wage? No, they think it belongs to them! We look after them like our own family, but they consider us rivals. Communists have put dangerous ideas into the heads of the untouchables. Now, they fight elections against us. These people have been the first victims of communism because they are totally uneducated. They do not worry about the unmaskable stench of cooking snails and sweat that drowns their living quarters, making their *cheri* stink from a mile away. But they *are* fixated with the red flag.

'Our downfall started when the first red flag went up twenty-five years ago. That's when the devil got into these people and they were brainwashed and made to believe in bloodshed.

'They are set on the path of violence. And that is why they are our enemies. They are bastards of the British.

These comrades are wanted criminals here, but where do they get the support from? London Parliament!'

Gopalakrishna Naidu pauses and looks around. Everyone avoids his eye. 'As it is, even our government does not deal with them with sufficient firmness and force. Only six months ago, the Communists cracked down on every village and beat up the coolies and small farmers who were loyal to us. What did the police do? What could be done anyway? They are useless. Did anyone care when the Communists killed Sub-Inspector Somasekhara Pillai? The police only beat a hasty retreat. For their own safety, they will turn a blind eye to the atrocities of the Communists. We cannot entrust a nincompoop like Inspector Rajavel to protect us. We are forced to bring not only labour from outside, but also bodyguards from elsewhere.'

He stops, acknowledges with pride his agent, Murthy, who controls his finances, imports his labourers and supplies his bodyguards. Quickly making sure that the momentum has not been lost, Gopalakrishna Naidu continues his tirade. 'These Communists are coming down upon us like the god of death – they are waging a full-fledged war. We should be strong. We should not budge from our stand. Now, they are fighting for even higher wages. Every six months they want it revised, and they are winning. We should be clear in telling them that we are not ready to be blackmailed into paying them more and more.

We should stop being scared of their strikes. Saying "no" with deep conviction is better than saying "yes" merely to avoid trouble. We should be firm. Remember, you can fine them, you can fire them. Buckling to their pressure out of fear betrays all of us.'

And to keep his Congress credentials intact, he also quotes Gandhi: 'It is better to be violent, if there is violence in our hearts, than to put on the cloak of non-violence to cover impotence.'

Carried away, like dry leaves in a strong wind, the men in the room cannot question his call to arms. He always gets what he wants, and what he wants now is complete surrender. Ramanuja Naidu's folded hands and Ganapati Nadar's downcast eyes are demure proof of that submission.

Gopalakrishna Naidu gets up.

He will soon drive away, leaving the other landlords shamefaced and speechless. Right now, they are all standing in silence. Not one of them can leave before their leader has left. This moment of stillness cries for closure.

So, do we drop the curtain here, on the inscrutable faces of the landlords? As you may have guessed, or possibly know from bitter experience, first-time novelists are highly predictable. It is the tedium of working in a dramatic medium. Even the few of them who have no faith in grand, delusional opening lines are suckers for sentiment when asked to come up with exit lines for their villains. So, let us hear Gopalakrishna Naidu one last time.

Standing at the threshold, he feels the envy in their eyes burn his back. He turns around to cast a disapproving glance at his fellow landlords. Lacking a moustache to twirl, he strokes his chin and says, 'If you can't be men, wear bangles.'

4. *Seasons of Violence*

Carrying the tales of their cunts and their cuntrees and their cuntenants, women cross all hurdles, talk in circles, burst into tears, break into cheers, teach a few others, take new lovers, become earth mothers, question big brothers, breathe state secrets, fuck all etiquette and turn themselves into the truth-or-dare pamphleteer who will interfere at the frontier. And in these rap-as-trap times, they perceive the dawn of the day and they start saying their permitted say.

So, when there is an old landowner who is a bad money-lender, they don't sit still, they start the gossip mill. And it is the holy writ: women don't crib on shit, 'cause they don't ask for it. The logic is clear: he looked for trouble, now they'll burst his bubble. They bitch without a hitch; speak non-stop like monsoon frogs. Then they plot their foolproof plan, they make their effigy man.

This is how the season of protest began.

*

Now, the Nicki Minaj within the novelist must be laid to rest. When the story gets a life of its own and gallops away recklessly, one must remind her of the rules: 'You don't try to steal in your dumbass mothafucking poetry into a goddamn historical novel, crazy bitch.' And so the critics decide that they should put certain, difficult questions before this undisciplined narrator. They act upon their urge to make the stupid hoe sit down for a Q&A session. Here is how it goes:

Why can't you fucking follow chronology?
I can. If you observe carefully, you will not fail to note that everyone gets fucked in due course of time.

Why can't you follow a standard narrative format?
If the reader wants a straight, humourless version of the events that surrounded the single biggest caste atrocity in India, she will read a research paper in the *Economic and Political Weekly* or a balanced press report. If the reader wants to understand the myriad landowning patterns in the Tanjore district, she will read an academic treatise like 'Rural Change in Southeast Asia' to find the ready-reckoner, drop-down list of hierarchies:

Landlords
– *Mirasdars*
– *Minors* (only used for *mirasdars* who wear too much gold jewellery and are proven womanizers)
Rich Peasants
Middle Peasants
Tenant Cultivators
Farm Overseers

And, at the bottom of the list, the four kinds of landless labourers:

Hereditary Serfs
– *Velaikkaarar* (servants)
– *Pannaiyal* (bonded permanent serfs)
Hired Labourers
– Regular Coolies
– Casual Coolies.

In another essay, Professor Gough will say that formerly, in Tanjore, all the Brahmins were *mirasdars*, and all the untouchables were landless labourers. The education will be immediate, procedural and perfect; it will not display any of the haughty haphazardness of this novel. After such class-based classification, the reader will encounter many intermediary castes: *Vellalar*, *Naidu* or *Naicker*, *Agamudaiyar*, *Mudaliar*, *Chettiar*, *Reddiyar*, *Konar*, *Kallar*,

Vanniyar, *Nadar*. She will be plagued by the plight of the untouchable castes: *Pallar*, *Paraiyar*, *Chakkiliyar*. The reader will be lost in such an alphabet soup. She will learn that life in these parts operates along lines of caste, and not just along structured feudal relations governing the modes of production. A reader cannot challenge what she does not comprehend. Beyond history lessons, she will find herself gravitating towards twisted tales. Hence, this rabble-rousing. Hence, this troublemaking. This craving for unintelligibility is a curse upon the postcolonial reader who seeks me out. And I write for my readers.

Will this chapter tell the story of the intervening months, July to December?
Yes. The way *Science* or *Nature* tells the story of every individual lab rat. This chapter is the most clinical in this book in that it actually borders on research. This is where the particulars are generalized to produce a reliable narrative.

Is there a single story?
No. Of course, I've consulted Chimamanda on this too.

Can every story be told?
Yes. I could do it if you were in the mood to read about how every landlord screwed the life of every labourer. Right now, I am concentrating on one story.

Were atrocities made into templates?
No. Not at all. That would be atrocious. It is just that being jerks, these feudal bastards did not have the fiction writer in mind and therefore they performed the same kinds of atrocities. Once in a while it totally went out of hand but, otherwise, addicted to their trademark morbidity, they lacked imagination.

Are you writing for writers?
No. Writers who read are readers firstly.

Should we wait for a better writer to tell this story?
No. And yes. Irrespective of your decision, I have decided to tell this story. And once I am done with this, there are other stories waiting to be told. And can you now please move away, so that I can address my readers?

*

For all my shortcomings, I will not force you to follow any linear or non-linear logic where hate travels along a lattice-bridge and arrives at a predestined location. I suspect hate is haphazard, with a mind of its own, and a reckless impatience that prevents it from charting its own course with flowcharts. Even if we stylistically try and recreate the texture of every other old-maid's tale, we must remember that hate is not always obedient to plot. It has ambition, it believes in unlimited possibilities and places its trust in tangents. And yet, we need to make peace, seek out the order in the chaos, the regularity in the randomness. That is why it is easier if you see some underlying formula that anchors you to the last vestiges of actuality. It would be better than making you chase every story on the caste violence unleashed on the untouchables in every *cheri* in every village. So, let us begin the quantification. I am giving you some options so that we formulate an atrocity-plot-generator for the East Tanjore district. All you will have to do is pick and choose. Never mind your own erratic choices, real news would have been far more frightening.

Attacking Force
Police, Paddy Producers Association, Landlords, Landlord-employed rowdies

Chief of Command
Name of Inspector, Name of Landlord

Nature of Atrocity
Looting, Rampaging, Whipping, Rape, Murder, Burning homes, Mass arrest

Extent of Damage
Deaths, Rapes, Hospital admissions, Homes burnt, Items stolen, Livestock missing

Ruse for Attack
Protest, Assertion, Refusal to join PPA, Activities of Communist Party, Convenient excuse Number Five, and so on

Victims
Women, Men, Children

Venue
Name of *cheri*

Date and Time, etc.

All that needs to be done now is filing a newspaper report. You have everything right here. Spend some time over that lead paragraph, please. And, yes, don't forget that inverted triangle format. Yes, yes, the chopping. Depends on the photos that we will run with it. Yes, yes, the captions have to be written. I will take care of it. Keep me posted.

Coming back to this chapter, the rest of *this* story that does not go into *your* story hangs like a snake around my throat. I am tired of the way it keeps moving in circles. I am afraid that it will never allow me the space for annotations. I have to surrender everything to someone else, someone on the outside. I am content with writing; the readers can do the commentary. This is how one turns readers into great pillow sobbers like Messers Socrates, Plato and Aristotle. Period, place and people.

Shall we get started?
Yes. It is important to engage.

When women take to protest, there is no looking back. This time it is the tractors. This time it is a Polydol death. This time it is a disappearance. This time it is a strike for higher wages. This time it is the demand for punishment for a rapist – the issues come and go and come again. Sometimes their demands are related to women alone, like when they demanded daily wages instead of the weekly wage for women. Or when they demanded their right to take breaks to attend to their infants, because babies left under the shade of trees cried to their death in their makeshift sari cradles, or rolled over and drowned in the mud. Most of the time, they fight for everybody. Once they smashed pots to protest their poor wages. Once, when the Paddy Producers Association put up its yellow flag in their village, they hauled it down, set fire to it and broke the flagpost. Once they went to the fields to harvest in the middle of the night, saying that they alone would harvest the crops they sowed, and that the landlords had no business employing outside labour. They are arrested for such transgressions, and because the police are such a benevolent force, they arrest the infants, too. The jails are full of fighting Madonnas. They are not afraid. They are not afraid of arrests. They are not afraid of hurt. On any given day, they can outweep the wailing police sirens. The women are adept at all of this: for the last three years, they have been stopping every job-stealing tractor in its tracks, standing in front of it, screaming the choicest abuses. The landlords punish these shrill-voiced women by stripping them almost naked and tying them to trees and whipping them in front of the whole village. The police punish them by making them kneel and walk a few miles on their knees until they have no choice but to crawl. But nothing breaks them. They are bold beyond the bruised skin and the bleeding knee.

Since the stage is set, the stuntmen move in. The fear of violence makes the people of the *cheri* flee. The landlords lead from the front lines. They take turns in their attacks, a code of honour that allows them to swap and circulate their rowdies and create uniform dread. They select the poorest *cheris* in their spheres of influence and pillage them. When they are on the rampage, they see no shame in looting from their own servants. They take away the goats and chickens and the brass vessels and all the small scraps of paper money that the women have carefully hidden inside. They steal all the stores of paddy. Sometimes, just out of spite, they burn roofs and clothes and they even spill the little salt they find. When the people of the *cheri* return, they are forced to start all over again.

When such things happen, the knee-jerk reaction of the people of the *cheri* is to go to the police. But they know that the policemen also practise untouchability: they have seen how the police have filed false cases against them, how the police are nothing but a private army on the payroll of the landlords, how the police are waiting for their own revenge. The police, as puppets of the ruling classes, will not make the law work for the poor. So the people go to the party. Depending on the grievousness of the situation, the party sends out petitions, pastes posters, organizes public meetings and stages protests.

Police raids on the *cheri* are timed affairs. Pre-dawn heist, operation high-noon, or the late-night show: when the people are unprepared and can be swooped down upon and stashed into police trucks. Today the vans of the Madras Special Police come and pick up all the able-bodied men in this *cheri*. They will be able to return home three months later. Today, the Kisan Deputy Superindent of Police at Tanjore decides to send policemen to stand guard on the imported labourers anywhere in the district. Today, the local police handcuff the local Communist leader and drag him through the village as if he were an animal, as if this would frighten the people away from the red flag. This keeps the people away from the police. This draws them closer to the party.

How not to expect militancy from men who wake up before sunrise, wear nothing more than a loincloth, walk in line every daybreak, wash their faces from any puddle of water, brush their teeth with red brick and are the colour of the earth they work? How not to expect anger from women whose friendliest banter involves swearing to cut off each other's cunts? How long will a people hold their patience when they earn their daily meal after sunset and have to hurry home to drop the handfuls of paddy into smouldering ash, wait for its wetness to waft away and then pound the grains and cook the dehusked rice into a formless congee that is never enough to douse their endless hunger? How can there be satisfaction, contentment, pleasure or the pursuit of happiness when women have to wake up every morning with a prayer that there is some tamarind, some dried chilli and half an onion in the home, anything to make the burning, red-hot chutney that can be licked from their fingers to let them tolerate the tastelessness of the leftover rice? Could the sight of a copper coin every week soften these women's curses? Just because they are paid *kalluk-kaasu*, a regular ration for drinking arrack, would their men give up on anger? In a land where the bullock walks of its own accord to the paddy field an hour in advance of sunrise, how long will it take before the men and women decide that they are not cattle, that they can break away, break free from their bondage, instead of hauling themselves to the field with a lantern in one hand and a sickle in the other? Could a people be silenced by not allowing them to even store the seeds of their labour, by denying them the yields of their harvest? When starvation stares them in the face, do they forget to speak?

The Communists know that the police have sworn to shoot them like dogs. They know the witch hunt that awaits them. They know the perils of the underground. They have to fight several forces: the landlords, the landlords' rowdies and henchmen, the police, the caste mentality that divides the working classes, the slackness of their party's high command, the gossip that threatens to ruin the years of hard work. They are proud of the memory of their BSR, B. Srinivasa Rao, the Brahmin comrade who mingled castelessly, the tall man who spoke to the landlords in English too and asked them such biting questions that if there had been any sense of shame in their blood, these *mirasdars* would have pulled out their own tongues and died. They are proud of their comrades who have killed landlords and lived to tell the tale. They are happy that the people no longer run thirty miles at the sight of a police uniform. They compete with movements that talk of self-respect and movements that talk of charity. They are worried about the militant communism of Naxalites, who want to annihilate every class enemy and bathe in their blood. They move against the politics of mercy and the politics of identity. They talk about the instruments of production, the nature of class struggle, the power of the proletariat. They explain the antagonism between the oppressed and the oppressing classes. It is not talk alone. They intervene when the landlords force a tenant farmer or a coolie labourer to place their black fingerprints on blank white paper. They want to ensure that the bright black grease of burnt hay and oil that slathers axle-rods of bullock carts can no longer be bartered for a man's freedom. The comrades promise a revolution they have never seen. They await a revolution that has been promised to them. They dream of red flags everywhere. But they know, too, how chopped up the party is. They know the lines of control. They know that they belong to the agricultural union that is affiliated to the Communist Party of India (Marxist). It is a matter of pride. It is also a matter of limits. They always have to speak to the centre, wait and talk back again. Negotiations at the higher levels involve diplomatic parleys and tacit understanding – ideology is a grim word in that paradise. For all their limited agency, the local Communist leaders face false cases every day. These comrades quote the letters of Jenny Marx verbatim to their wives when asked to justify their poverty. They tell themselves to keep their trust in the people.

When the labourers went on strike, they went hungry. When hunger got the better of them, they went to the landlords to work out a deal. Sometimes, as it happens now, the labourers are bound by their collective decision not to work, and the landlords are bound by their collective decision not to employ. At first, the landlords hurl abuse. They make do with imported labour, bringing in men and women from the famine-hit areas of Ramnad. But the peasant struggle spreads like an infection, it catches the landlords unawares, takes them on from unsuspecting quarters. The threat of a protracted fight brings the landlords to the negotiation table. The proletariat is united and powerful and radiantly angry, but the landlords gain strength from the guns they carry. The landlords know that the comrades know that at least six men would have to die before they are close enough to attack a gun-wielding *mirasdar*. Fear of facing the bullets prevents a spontaneous blood bath. So protests take democratic forms: hunger strikes, hartals and road rokos, demonstrations and processions.

The protests also take dramatic forms. Now a landlord has finished off their charismatic leader and the people do not know what became of his body. This time they have not been given jobs, and outside labour has been employed. This time a landlord cheats them out of their rightful wages. This time a landlord has instructed the shopkeepers not to sell anything to the people of the *cheri*. This time, in protest, they plan a funeral for the landlord. They prepare his pyre, they lament his effigy corpse on its final farewell.

The women beat their breasts and break their bangles. They sing the dirges of disgust, they mourn a monster, who, being alive, understands what awaits him after death. They curse, and it is written in their blood that their curses will come true. They call upon death to visit him at the earliest and, sometimes, the Buffalo Rider keeps his appointment. When women take to protest, there is no looking back.

5. *Marxist Party Pamphlet*

Dear Comrades, Brothers and Sisters,

RED SALUTE!

Harvest is the season where patriotic myths come to die. It is the season when pacts are flouted, working people are hounded and Communist cadres are killed by the landlords. The murder of our comrade, SIKKAL PAKKIRISAMY, in broad daylight on 15th November 1968, is not an isolated incident that should spark anger and tension only in Nagapattinam.

On the contrary, it concerns everyone.

One must be reminded that the landlords had him killed on the day of the agricultural strike in East Tanjore, during the public procession, in order to spread terror among the peasants and labourers.

When people in the big cities read such news, they easily dismiss it and do not even question why these murders take place.

Comrade Gramsci, one of the greatest Communist

intellectuals, wrote about the emotional paralysis of our society: 'As a collective they are not disturbed by the painful spectacles that are presented to them. As a collective they don't faint when the still-breathing corpse of a murdered child is thrown at their feet. The commotion that every individual has felt, the heartache, the sympathy that every individual has felt, has not scratched the granite-like compactness of the social class.'

These words were never more true.

There are a few people who, on an individual level, agree that the agricultural labourers live under dire circumstances, that they do not own a foothold of land, that they are mired in debt, that they lose their young children to starvation and their elderly to disease because of a lack of sufficient food and medicine. When these people hear about the plight of the coolies, they cluck with sympathy, but do they dream of change? Why do they react with complacency when they come across news of the broad-daylight murder of a comrade who worked all his life for the poorest of the poor? Do they not realize that it is their duty to stand in support of these oppressed workers? Do they not realize that a strike is not an act of disobedience alone, but an act of resistance? Even if they realize, they will merely stay silent and go about their own work. Why? They are held back by fear, they are held back by selfishness. But, one day, they will pay the price of their silence.

The tragedy around us will affect them too and, one day, they will understand the importance of supporting the proletarian struggle. That day they will stop believing the false propaganda of the ruling classes. That day, they will know the true people's history. It is not a history that is available in the police records or the newspapers. It is not a history that textbooks will teach, or a history that will catch the attention of petty bourgeois writers. But it is a history that we must learn, a history that will set us free, a history that we can harvest.

Communism teaches the people and opens their eyes, gives them the strength to defend themselves, makes them realize their own power, tells them the importance of devoting time for the cause of revolution. Today, we are able to hold meetings, print posters, gather for rallies and hoist our red flag with pride because of the sustained and single-minded devotion with which our comrades have built the cadre base of the party among the proletariat.

It was almost impossible in the beginning. To meet people in the dead of night, to disperse well before daybreak, to talk to them about their troubles, to tell them the history of revolutionary struggles. The British banned all meetings of the peasant unions under the Defence of India Act. That did not deter us. In those early days, we trained the people to think fearlessly. We gave them courage in the face of danger and our leaders taught them the martial art of *silambattam*, so that they could defend themselves. Alas! Even the sounds of the clashing sticks would arouse suspicion and the landlords would launch yet another inquisition to check if communism had made any inroads into their territory. Death was often the prize if a Communist was discovered by a landlord, and public disgrace if he was discovered by the police.

Those were the days when the party's secret meetings were held in cremation grounds. We used to get away with it because the informers dismissed the light of our torches as the fire-breathing tongue of the *kollivaai pisaasu*. But we managed to take the message of Marxism to the masses. How else would this world know about the rapes and murders of agricultural workers that take place behind the fifteen-foot-high compound walls of landlords? The same landlords who massacre a whole village and walk away with honours? Who else fought against the system of feudal slavery, where husbands were asked to whip their wives if they slacked at work, or spoke back to their masters?

The Kalappal Agreement was the first landmark victory in our struggle. As the working people rallied around the Communists, the landlords were forced to strike a compromise. This deal fixed the daily wage at two measures of paddy and opened the door to an increase in the harvest wages. Today, this agreement is famous because it was the first to put an end to the cruel practice of whipping and the forceful feeding of *saanippaal* to labourers as punishment. The agricultural labourers were represented by our comrades Amirthalingam, Rajagopal and Kuppusamy, the legendary Kalappal Kuppu.

The second major agreement that came about because of Communist intervention was the Mannargudi Agreement, made between striking agricultural workers and their landlords. Signed in the presence of Tanjore district collector, Ismail Khan – a very good man as our comrades say – the deal guaranteed that the daily wage would be raised to three measures and that the labourers were entitled to a one-seventh share of the harvest. It also made it mandatory for landlords to use standardized measures to pay the labourers and provide a receipt to the local authorities giving details of the total harvest.

Who worked hard, who fought to stop the old convention of making the agricultural labourers work from sunrise to sunset, and instead fixed a day as six in the morning to six in the evening? It was the Communist Party that first succeeded in securing a holiday for the agricultural labourers. The six-day work week might be famous on government calendars, but the poor peasants were not entitled to any such break. When the early Communists campaigned for a day's break, they had to go on strike. Finally, every *amavasai* day was made a holiday because we demanded that the labourers should at least have the right to remember their dead ancestors.

The Mannargudi Agreement was signed on 25 December 1944, but nearly a quarter-century later, what have we achieved? Though we have a rich history and a long connection to communism, with the Madras Labour Union being the oldest in India, we have not been able to make significant advancement. We still continue to sign agreements with the landlords. We still have not achieved our dream of land redistribution.

In Tanjore district, the area known as the granary of South India, Vadapathimangalam Thiagaraja Mudaliar owns 15,000 acres of land; Kunniyur Subramania Iyer and Sambasiva Iyer own 5,000 acres each; Rao Bahadur Subburathna Mudaliar owns 2,500 acres; KG Estates owns 4,000 acres, KTV Estates owns 3,000 acres and K. C. Desikar owns 15,000 acres. This is not a Communist Party statistic; it is extracted from a report prepared by the World Bank, that crony of the imperialist powers. It is evident to everybody that land in Tanjore is monopolized by a few individuals. The working people have no lands; those who till the soil have no rights. Peasants are being treated worse than slaves. To talk of land distribution here is to talk of the gross inequality that sustains the feudal structure. To put it in simple numbers, 60 per cent of the land lies with 5 per cent of the people at the top; at the bottom, 60 per cent of the people own only 5 per cent of the land. And below this are the wretched of the earth: the landless agricultural labourers of Tanjore, who own nothing, not even the land on which their tiny, mud-walled huts stand, not even metal vessels, not even a change of clothing. And it is the rights of these have-nots, these proletarians, that the Paddy Producers Association seeks to crush. Though their powers have been eroded by years of our unrelenting struggle, they enjoy immunity because of their political connections.

When the agricultural labourers protested against the utilization of tractors in East Tanjore, the state provided security to the landlords by drafting in its police force. But, comrades, one day sooner or later, the words of our great leader Marx will come true and, as he said, the working people will direct their attacks not against the bourgeois conditions of production, but against the instruments of production themselves. They will destroy imported wares that compete with their labour, they will smash to pieces machinery, they will set factories ablaze, they will seek to restore by force the vanished status of the workman.

The landlords have learnt how to quell our protests. They appoint a police force of fifty men and a rowdy force of fifty men to protect every tractor. What can be done in such a situation?

A year ago, we launched a poster campaign so that people would stay brave and have the courage to tackle the police. We did not want our women to shudder at the sight of a uniform. We designed a poster to directly attack them: 'Police Dogs! Cause Trouble and You Will Pay Double!' These posters appeared all over the district: Mannargudi, Thiruthuraipoondi, Vedaranyam, Nagapattinam, Mayawaram, Kumbakonam, Sirkazhi. The police, in shock over such an open attack, alleged in their special reports that these posters had been dropped by the Soviet Union with the help of a silent aeroplane. This is an indication of the extent of their imagination. The ruling classes are aware of the benefits of propaganda to ensure that the people are estranged from the Communist parties.

As a result of such propaganda, people are unable to distinguish truth from falsehood. They believe these cock-and-bull stories of the government; they believe that trade unions and strikes by the labourers cause all the problems; they are unaware of the scores of young children who are dying from hunger every day. The middle class, just like the ruling class, conveniently believes that those who die are the surplus people, the ones who took up space, the nation's disgrace. Does the middle class have enough of a conscience to feel rattled when, every time the monsoon fails, the parched lands grow soup kitchens?

We take this opportunity to remind the chief minister that the previous Indian National Congress government was kicked out of power because of famine and starvation.

The proletariat will never forgive a tyrant who forces them to bury their children. You are in power only because your party's election manifesto promised one measure of rice for one rupee.

In fact, this Dravida Munnetra Kazhagam (DMK) government has overseen the most difficult year of the last decade. Every time a mill has shut shop, workers have been forced to flee to other states in search of employment. Workers are striking in rubber plantations, paper mills, rice mills, sugar mills, textile mills. To date, twenty-seven cotton mills have been closed, rendering 20,000 weavers jobless and bringing their families to absolute penury. Teaching and non-teaching staff have not been paid for months in several colleges across the state. Schoolchildren are forced to go without midday meals in several districts. There is not a single class of people that has not been affected by the mishandling and incompetence of the present government. In all the cities, there is water shortage. Cholera and malaria are touching alarming levels.

The bitter truth is, we have an undeclared famine. In the southern districts, rationing is hitting the poor, who are getting less and less from the public distribution system. People who were entitled to 1,200 grams of food grain per week are now being allowed only a maximum of 800 grams. This is a one-third cut in consumption that the government has gifted to the people. Being the wonder that is India, we also hear reports of fire destroying food-grain storage godowns. Only a fool will fail to see the hand of money-hungry landlords behind these acts of arson.

In this dire situation, moneylending in villages has become deplorable, with rates of interest ranging from 50 to 300 per cent. The poor have no recourse but to further enslave themselves in these circles of debt.

At least as a humanitarian gesture, the government loan collection could have been postponed. But when does the government act with the proletariat in mind?

Only an extremely heartless and perversely well-entrenched government can be unmoved on hearing of the atrocities of untouchability that are committed against the Adi Dravidar agricultural labourers in our Tanjore district. The landlords build a cement shelter for their cows, but these people have to huddle under a blanket of night sky because they are considered 'untouchable'. Even worse, the greed of these landlords is killing the poor workers. In the last two years, at least three men have died in every large farm because of the poisonous effects of spraying Polydol. They have died in the field, hospital, or en route, and while it is clear that these deaths occurred because of chemical pesticides, the government has not taken a single step to prevent them from occurring, it has not issued any stern warning to the landlords and it has even not paid any compensation to the families of these victims. Instead, it has maintained its comprador-bourgeois character and continues the import of these poisonous pesticides in order to bring about its promise of a 'Green Revolution'.

We have been swindled in the name of gods, in the name of religion, in the name of caste. Now, we are being swindled in the name of development.

Comrades, we will be making a grave blunder if we assume that everything that is happening in the delta district is merely a local problem. Was it just drought and defective distribution that caused the food crisis? Even American imperialism needs to shoulder its share of the burden of guilt. Using the ruse of the Indo-Pak War, America delayed shipment of food grains, and we sank into famine. America is interested in the Green Revolution because it seeks to prevent the Red Revolution.

In the name of this Green Revolution, we are dependent on American fertilizers. In Tanjore district alone, the use of fertilizer has had a 2,000 per cent increase. This is not healthy. We have seen in every village alcoholics who can only walk steadily when they are drunk. Our land has become addicted to these chemical fertilizers in the same manner – if she does not have her fill, she forgets her fertility. She stops bearing crops. The government does not care because these projects fill its coffers.

Let us not forget what this DMK government has said. Although they could never have ousted the Indian National

Congress without the support of the Communist parties and the intense door-to-door campaigning undertaken by our cadres in every tiny hamlet, they have betrayed us. Karunanidhi has boldly proclaimed that the Communists will be crushed with an iron fist. They have made a pact with the ruling classes. They have no sense of shame in promoting feudal tyrants to occupy positions of power in their party. All the laws have been framed by the government only to protect the ruling classes and to safeguard their political and economic interests. Just as the Pannaiyal Protection Act brought bonded agricultural servants to the streets and made them mere daily-wage earning coolies, the Land Ceiling Act has proved to be another ploy to secure the interests of the ruling classes. We know of an instance where a landlord in Tanjore set up sixteen trusts to manage thousands of acres of temple land, and then these lands were leased out to tenants, all of whom happened to be his hereditary slaves, his domestic servants, his barber and his cook and his book-keeper and their children. On paper, they were in charge of the land but, in practice, they continued to do the same menial chores, absolutely unaware of what they were materially worth.

Our cadres – no, indeed, the whole of Nagapattinam – lost all respect for the DMK when Chief Minister Annadurai came to unveil the statue of Vengadangal Naidu, a landlord infamous for his atrocities against women and the 'untouchable' castes. The landlord sharks here came together under his leadership and the banner of the Paddy Producers Association. Their only common goal is to harass the agricultural labourers, deprive them of all their rights and drive them deeper and deeper into misfortune. The oppressed 'untouchable' castes, who form the majority of the working-class peasantry, have no security. They have no right to any type of social justice.

The government is not doing anything to help matters. Indiscriminate police shooting and lathi charges have now become commonplace. The police have attacked peaceful processions staged by workers in Nellikuppam and Neyveli. If this is the state of affairs in northern Tamil Nadu, one cannot even begin to imagine the high-handedness of the police in southern Tamil Nadu. They are guests of the *mirasdars*, they feast on the mutton curry cooked in their honour, and behave as if they were nothing but a private uniformed army. The atrocities committed by the policemen against the women labourers are so savage that they cannot even be written down. The police force has become a pack of hunting dogs that the government unleashes on any dissenting force.

But the working masses have been unfazed in facing this brutality of the state machinery that has always acted at the behest of the feudal structure. Our comrades have filled up jails with joy with the knowledge that their suffering today will ensure a better life for the entire world tomorrow. The red flag rests in revolutionary hands.

Revolutions and uprisings have toppled dictators, they have sounded the death knell of oppression! This is not the time to sit at the sidelines. This is not the time to be a spectator. This is the time to take to the streets. This is the time for the workers of the world to unite. Comrades, let us never forget that the future will only contain what we put into it now!

The district-level agricultural workers' demonstration to be held on 26 November at Nagapattinam bus-stand is meant to show the huge opposition that exists to the pro-feudal, pro-imperialist activities of the state government. The Marxist party wants to condemn the violence unleashed against our cadres, most recently the cold-blooded murder of party leader SIKKAL PAKKIRISAMY on 15 November. No action has been taken, and even though the entirety of Nagapattinam knows that the man responsible for his murder is Vinayagam Naidu of the DMK, the police force, under the instructions of the DMK high command, has not arrested anybody. On the other hand, police have increased their atrocities against our party, and they have threatened to order a blanket ban on all our meetings, rallies and demonstrations. They refuse to understand that the anger of the proletariat will rectify every injustice in this world. We should be angry that we are not angry enough.

We have not been able to save the life of our comrade, although we knew about the grave threats he faced from the Paddy Producers Association. Even our alacrity could not prevent his murder at the hands of Vinayagam Naidu. We stayed together day and night, we slept at the party office in Nagapattinam, and we stayed like each other's shadows. Alas! We have lost one of our most popular grassroots workers who organized the people. They attacked him in the blink of an eye and we no longer have this brave and committed comrade with us. His murder was the result of a deal between Vinayagam Naidu and Gopalakrishna Naidu – a division of labour – the former wanted to finish off his biggest threat, and the latter has taken upon himself the task of forcing the people of Kilvenmani to abandon the red flag, an end for which he is willing to adopt any means. Our appeals to the police and the chief minister to provide protection to the people of Kilvenmani have fallen on deaf ears.

This must not go unopposed. The Paddy Producers Association must be banned for the sake of democracy. We need all possible support and solidarity for our strikes. Let us show our strength in Nagapattinam. Let us stand shoulder to shoulder with the people of Kilvenmani and tell them that they are not alone. The proletariat rallying together can be the biggest homage that we can pay to our slain comrade, SIKKAL PAKKIRISAMY! Let us pay our red salutes to him by putting an end to the atrocities of the murderous PPA landlords!

Red flag shall triumph!
Long live communism!
Long live revolution!

6. *Oath of Loyalty*

Police Constable Muthupandi; Gopalakrishna Naidu's nameless-for-the-purpose-of-this-novel cook; and the official party organ of the Communist Party of India (Marxist) share the uniform opinion that the agricultural workers' demonstration held to pay homage to Comrade Sikkal Pakkirisamy attracted more than 3,000 people. More than 300 policemen were deployed to ensure that this public rally passed off peacefully.

These facts, plain and unadorned, will be rejected by those readers whose minds have been poisoned by the passion of the novel. Such injured souls – as a certain Mr Thomas Jefferson observed – carry a bloated imagination, sickly judgment and disgust towards all the real businesses of life. They are not going to be dazzled by date and time and location. They will not give in to name and place and all the greasy, gratifying noun-fuck that gives one the aura of authenticity. If they want a linear narrative and a self-contained story, they will read the day's newspaper, not a novel. Being in the business of entertaining such disturbed minds, I shall don the mantle of devious author, and set about my job of disorienting the reader.

Now, the readers-at-large don't know what exactly happened between the murder on 15 November and the massacre on 25 December 1968. They can find the dateline in an excellent documentary on this subject, *Ramayyahvin Kudisai*, but asking them to rush to their nearest video library is not a good way to fill up a first novel. Sitting here in Canterbury, with video footage of the village ready to run continuously for five solid days, and with four diaries bristling with notes, I shall surmise and theorize, assume and presume, speculate and conflate and extrapolate every detail revealed by my field research in order to make it fit into the narrative mode of my novel. The age of apologizing authors is long gone.

Let me follow the format of the previous page.

A villager asked to face a handheld video-cam for the first time, a reporter writing his in-depth opinion piece on this subject in under 1,000 words, and a novelist sorting out her storyline, will tell you with an air of certainty that Comrade Sikkal Pakkirisamy's murder on the day of the district-level agriculture strike proved to be a flashpoint for the tragedy that followed. They will not begin their story with the arrival of the various Europeans, or the story of rice cultivation in this delta district, or the local kings' largesse and land grants to the Brahmins, or the history of local invasions, or the emergence of communism, or the shrill independence movement, or the manner in which Murugan first manifested himself to the divine in their dreams and then had a temple built in his honour and for his worship, or the origins of untouchability that set apart and put aside some men and some women, or the succour offered by the slave trade of the brown peoples, or the anti-God activities of the Self-Respect Movement or the establishment of the first church at Tranquebar or the formation of the peasant associations or the foundation of the Paddy Producers Association, because it would be easy to get caught up in this multi-dimensional mess of events and impossible to pull oneself out of these knots. Unlike this jumble that is beyond disambiguation, the selection of a key incident such as the murder of Sikkal

Pakkirisamy removes the creases from the timeline. Like a lullaby, it transports us to a safe zone in time so that when we wake up, we can discuss this historical tragedy with the same self-assuredness that everybody employs when they speak of the assassination of Archduke Franz Ferdinand of Austria as being the immediate trigger that led to the First World War.

So, somewhere in this sultry chapter, we shall begin at the immediate beginning.

What is a story worth if it does not have a supernatural element? Why begin when you cannot bring in the gods?

On the day Jayabalan's mother-in-law dropped dead from starvation, a legislator in faraway Madras expressed concern about chronic food-grain scarcity, famine conditions and exorbitant prices; another took issue that cultivators in Tiruchy had been deprived of paddy for their own consumption as state revenue officials had forcibly procured all their harvest; the chief minister tabled a report on the extent of damage caused by a cyclone, along with a detailed break-down of the relief and rehabilitation measures undertaken by his government; while local temple-dweller Lord Murugan, popular in these parts under his alias of Sikkal Singaravelan, according to his strict daily regimen, was bathed in milk twice that morning, noon and night.

When he learnt, after his sixth bath, that the local Communist leader Sikkal Pakkirisamy had been killed off by the landlords, his lordship Sikkal Singaravelan prayed for his own safety – *Murugamurugamurugamurugamuruga-muruga* – and decided not to interfere in the internal affairs of this mad and murderous district. Although he was not bothered about the equitable distribution of resources or the wage struggle of the workers, his lordship knew that he was no different from the local Communist leader in two aspects: he always sought to be defined by his domain of influence, and he could put up a good show of strength at short notice. Being a bright young chap, he decided that he would not risk taking a position on anything outside his own war portfolio, as long as he was provided with food to eat and milk to drink so that he didn't drop dead and make two women instantaneous widows. He kept his word. He turned a blind eye to the blood baths.

Any student of history with access to Wikipedia will be able to tell you, with the requisite annotations, that in the 1968 winter session of the parliament of gods, he abstained from voting on every issue except Vietnam, where he enjoyed cult status as Saigon Subramaniam.

We cut to the chase. We jump past the murder scene. We display the novel through a series of rushed frames. We recreate the aftermath.

When news of the marked man being successfully hacked to death was conveyed to them, the landlords rejoiced and called for grand celebrations. They feasted on flesh, secure in the knowledge that a corpse that has gone to the burning ground does not return.

As demanded by chronological narrative and the rigours of routine, the landlords went to their fields the day after the agricultural strike. There, the much-anticipated twist lay in wait for them: none of the workers had turned up. Then it was revealed to them – in a discreet fashion as merits a novel of a certain literary quality – that every worker in Nagapattinam was away attending the funeral procession of Sikkal Pakkirisamy. As warranted by the mores of their social class at that time, they took it as a personal affront. They termed the two-day absence from work as arrogance and insolence and impudence and a Communist nuisance. They met together, called on each other, and decided to obey their leader. Naturally, as always happens in these novels and is sometimes reflected in real life, the landlords turned away the agricultural labourers who came to work the next day and demanded that they pay a fine.

Since mirroring is a major plot device, now it was the turn of the peasants to meet together, call on each other and decide to obey their party leader. And, incredible as it may seem to any reader, the Communists announced that they would not pay any fines and that they would go on an indefinite strike until they were allowed to work. As if not reporting to work was going to solve the problem of being ordered not to report for work!

Now that both sides are in a clear deadlock, the nail-biting reader can join the nervous author in elaborating the rest of the story.

Slowly the deadlock was unlocked. Some landlords relented after a token fine was paid. Some workers, dreading death by hunger, came to a compromise by discarding their party connections. Some others, petrified of the many horrors that would visit their village if they enraged the *mirasdars* any further, went to work.

As happens in stories of a similar nature, one village stood apart. Kilvenmani paid the token twenty-rupee fine for abstaining from work, but it didn't strike a deal, and it continued to strike. The one-day district-level strike had been marred by a murder, but their collective demand for higher wages was kept alive by Kilvenmani. Common sense and Communist thinking told them that their labour was indispensable in the harvest season. They expected the landlords to give in and grant them the daily wage of six measures of paddy they had been fighting for.

But the *mirasdars* saw no reason to relent.

Moving beyond the ensemble cast that has been employed for the purposes of the novel so far, the *mirasdars* simply brought in outside labour. The agents, exploitative and eager to please the landlords, transported labourers willing to work for a mere meal a day from Ramnad and other nearby districts, setting the strikers against the starving, the poor against the desperate. The police, so far relegated to the position of neutral observers, extended protection to these agents and their congee coolies. This, expectedly, made matters worse.

In order to move this narrative turn of events to its next level of complexity, let us assume that this loss of employment causes enormous hardship to the agricultural labourers, who appeal to the Communists to solve the problem, who petition the government to step into the matter, but nothing comes of it. So, at this point, where they appear to be losing, the Communists decide that enough is enough and hold a series of public meetings to garner support for the villagers of Kilvenmani. To maintain the element of balance, one has to concede that the Paddy Producers Association also held rival meetings. Things happened, but we need not give everything away right here in such a straightforward fashion.

What's a story without a strong voice, anyway?

Reader, now that you have swallowed the pulp, you can leave the peel intact. Trust your instincts to tell you the rest of the tale.

This is what Muthusamy the Communist and Muniyan the Headman and Ratnam the Communist Party secretary and Subban and Murugan and Karuppaiah and Palayam and Pandari Ramayya and Thangaraju and Natesan and Panikkan and Kaliyappan and Srinivasan and Jayabalan and Veerappan and Kathaiyan and Arumugam and Seppan and Thangavelu and Sellamuthu and Vairakannu and Veeraiyyan and Balakrishnan and Muni and Ratinasamy and Palanivelu and Ramalingam and Thayyan and Kannusamy and Marudaiyyan and Periyaan and Raman would have said – when questioned alone or as part of a group – about what transpired after the village of Kilvenmani had taken its oath of loyalty to the red flag.

Gopalakrishna Naidu ordered the owner of our village, Ganapati Nadar, who ordered his *pannaiyal* Subramanian, who asked our village head, who asked the people of our village and they said they would not obey. It was the people's decision and so our village stood by the red flag, fearless of the consequences. We decided there was no way the flag was going to be removed. We knew that it would save us. We knew that it would voice our demands. Any other flag had no business here. This information was relayed to Gopalakrishna Naidu. He went wild. He promised to burn our village and kill our people. He wanted to teach us a lesson. He wanted us to go hungry so that we would be forced to beg for food. He ordered that anybody from our village should not be given any job. We would go looking for jobs but all the landlords in East Tanjore had been told not to employ us if and when we came to them. Gopalakrishna Naidu had sent a messenger with a handwritten letter to all these landlords in the neighbouring villages in the district.

It was a suffering that we had never undergone so far. We went to where our sisters and cousins and aunts had been married away, under the guise of guests, but kept looking for any job that we could find. Only a handful of us stayed here. We would borrow rice or money or grain or lentils and come home and live here for a few days and then go to another relative's house and this is how we passed the time. Gopalakrishna Naidu had reduced us to slaves. We starved. The landlords did not give us work. They did not give us loans. It was a complete social boycott. We lived through those difficult days with hunger and fear and fortitude. The party told us that they did not have money, but they had the masses. What could we do? What could be done?

Words transform when they travel through a medium. They die, but worse, they can kill. In a novel like this, there is no point in shooting the messenger dead.

In the village of Kilvenmani, *pannaiyal* Subramanian is the link man. It is through him that the villagers pay the fine for abstaining from work; it is through him that they are ordered to join the PPA; it is through him that they are ordered to pay the fine for boycotting the PPA and for instead staying with the Communist Party and swearing by its red flag.

He speaks forwards and backwards.

Through him the village of Kilvenmani declines, and through him the village hears the voice of untrammelled arrogance. 'I have said what needs to be said and so there is nothing more to say.' It is through him that they receive their threats; it is through him that they learn that their end is near.

Like the fool of all folklore, this man will survive and stay unscathed.

The Paddy Producers Association's regular, endlessly repeated formula – threaten, beat up, force the labourer to leave the Communist Party – failed miserably in Kilvenmani. The ripple effect of terror that forced other villages to abandon the red flag did not shake this village. They continued to strike.

That is why the association decided to use blackmail tactics in Kilvenmani. It could be called into question for undemocratic practices and extrajudicial trouble-shooting methods, but the association stuck to its logical loops of threat, which were difficult to fault at first sight.

This was a collective decision taken by Ganapati Nadar, Muthukrishna Naidu, Narayanasamy Pillai, Ramu Thevar, Ramanuja Naidu and other *mirasdars* on behalf of Gopalakrishna Naidu. For the criminal transgression of participating in Sikkal Pakkirisamy's funeral procession and boycotting work the following day, it went beyond collecting the twenty-rupee fine, and it put forth a list of conditions:

Kilvenmani must leave the Communist Party.
Or else, they must pay a fine of Rs 250.
Or else, they must join the Paddy Producers Association.
Or else, they must face the consequences.
Or else.

In the midst of this drama, there is one scene that involves the surly priest, Sundaresa Gurukkal, making *sakkarai pongal*, the cloying feast of rice and jaggery at the Kali temple. The feast is sponsored by the princely sum of twenty rupees collected from the Kilvenmani villagers as punishment for being absent from work for two consecutive days. This money has been donated to the temple by the Paddy Producers Association. All the office-bearers partake of the *sakkarai pongal*.

This is utterly useless information at present, but it might come in handy at a later date. Try and remember this.

The elders of Kilvenmani are clear about certain things: we are not asking for the land. We are not asking for homes. We are asking for work because we need food. We are asking for food, for our six measures of paddy, because we are going hungry – because what we have, what we are getting paid, is not enough for our stomachs. We may die of starvation but until our demand is met, we are not giving up the strike.

Though their demand is just, it is ignored. Ganapati Nadar, Muthukrishna Naidu, Narayanasamy Pillai, the landlords who employed them previously, are ordered not to appeal on their behalf. The pimping-landlord, Ramasamy Porayar, and his son, have also been ordered not to employ anybody from Kilvenmani, not even the women.

Gopalakrishna Naidu's writ runs large. On the first full-moon day in December, his relative Kerosene Govinda summons five active party workers from Kilvenmani: Muthusamy, Muniyan, Natesan, Kaliyappan and Subramanian. And he is reported to have said: 'Your demand was conveyed but our president is very firm. He will not budge. He has asked me to collect this fine of Rs 250 from you for continuing to strike.'

Kilvenmani's representatives refuse to pay. They say that they cannot pay. They say that even when they harvest a sackful, they are paid only a pittance. Four and a half measures of paddy for every sack containing sixty measures. The women are paid even less.

They have a simple answer: 'You cannot ask us for a fine, you should not ask us for a fine, and even if you did ask us for a fine, we cannot pay. We simply don't have that kind of money.'

Then they are warned of the attack. They are told how angry Gopalakrishna Naidu is. Kerosene Govinda says that the only way to avoid trouble is to pay this fine. He knows, like everyone else, that this money is way beyond their reach, that even if all of the men and the women and the children in Kilvenmani went into the fields and worked and worked, it would take a few weeks for so much money to materialize. The fine is an excuse, a fine ruse, to shame the stubborn village.

The villagers go to another landlord, Ramanuja Naidu. He hears them out for an hour. And then, this time, power speaks in another language, but still addresses them with its characteristic arrogance. He tells them: Hoist the flag of the Paddy Producers Association. Remove the red flag. Report for work this instant.

That doesn't happen.

So, the Paddy Producers Association goes one step further. On 15 December, the association organizes a meeting in Kilvenmani itself. The meeting is held in the caste-Hindu street as a culmination of a public procession. Gopalakrishna Naidu presides over this Sunday gathering, and his henchmen are present in full strength. He publicly issues threats and warnings, he gives a ten-day deadline to Kilvenmani to reform itself and give up the red flag. His lawyers also perform in public: giving advice, giving threats. This show of strength scares the people of Kilvenmani. They are not amused.

The elders project rage because it helps them conceal unknown fears. They know that they are faced with a challenge. The entire *cheri* gathers in the coconut grove near Pandari Ramayya's home and discusses the issue: Should we surrender to the landlords? Should we continue with the red flag?

Everybody attends the meeting. The Pallars. The Paraiyars. The men, the women, the children. Even Arumugam, incapable of walking on his polio-withered legs, is there.

Some features of the village meeting were typical. Such as Jayabalan's two wives standing as far away from each other as possible. But, this time, the men did not do most of the talking.

Sundaram started it and set the tone when she complained of how she had to go and plead with Ramanuja Naidu and fall at his feet and beg his forgiveness and seek to reform herself and her family after his henchmen in Irukkai had burnt her husband's red towel and held him captive for three days. Finally, he was only freed after another roguish *mirasdar*, Ramu Thevar, had written a letter to Naidu saying that Veerappan had been a trusted servant whose grandfather had worked under his grandfather, and so on, and this intervention had spared her husband's life.

Then Muniyan's wife, Thangamma, said that two days ago her pregnant sister was pummelled by a gang of twenty armed men who were imported rowdies from Ramnad and possibly working for Gopalakrishna Naidu. To which Sethu said that one devil always outdid another because her friend, Anju, from the neighbouring village, had been waylaid by Chandran and eight others and they had torn apart her red blouse and burnt it before her eyes and beaten her up and nobody could even take her to the hospital for treatment because the landlord and his rowdies prevented that.

Pattu said this was a bad trend because the victims couldn't be taken to the hospital and the doctors wouldn't come to the *cheri*. And when Letchumi claimed that all the injured men were being treated only with turmeric, everyone nodded in agreement.

Paappa, heavily pregnant and full of stories that she culled from her friends, said that Rasathi of Velankanni had been attacked by a landlord, and the elders of her caste had decreed that he must seek her apology and bear her medical expenses, but the landlords had taken offence and crippled them through social boycotts and 200 men came in six tractors to rampage through the *cheri* and two days later Rasathi committed suicide by drinking Polydol, ashamed and afraid of all the evil that she would further bring upon her people.

And then they shared more stories.

And then these women said that if the men wanted their mothers and wives and sisters and daughters to live with some honour and dignity, they should stand by the Communists and continue to fight these rowdy landlords.

One can also safely assume that at this critical juncture, Muthusamy, the Communist Party leader in Kilvenmani, would have giddily quoted Comrade Sukumaran's favourite French Revolution quote – 'Those who make revolutions halfway only dig their own graves.' He had been saving up these words for a long, long time.

Any sociologists and other bored academics who may scour my novel for information about the sexual, alcoholic and deviant indulgences of my protagonists will be sorely disappointed. I am telling a story so that a story gets told, not with the intention that somebody, somewhere, is going to be awarded a PhD for studying the postmodern perversions of this novel. If you want to learn who was boozing that morning, who were the two lovers who stayed away from the village meeting for a secret rendezvous, or which was the one family that had switched its loyalty to Gopalakrishna Naidu, you won't find that information here.

Okay, curiosity is inevitable and I can understand why you would want to know at least some of the things said at the village meeting. Of course, you are aware of the fact that I was not there, so to make up these monologues-dialogues-speeches-soliloquies on demand causes great discomfort to me as a writer. Here are three snippets. Go ahead, paste your smiley faces on them.

Dialogue 1: Srinivasan, angered by his brother Subramanian being the go-between, threatened to stop talking to him if he kept pleading the case of the landlords. He is also said to have called Subramanian a *thodanadungi*, a Tamil insult that signalled way more derision than its literal translation: a man-with-twitching-thighs.

Dialogue 2: 'Bait does not become food,' Muthusamy said.

And in order to dangle a convincing explanation for his aphorism, he pointed out that everyone in the village would have witnessed first-hand the fate of the hungry fish who seeks to eat an easy worm. This fishy symbolism was not immediately understood because the people who were fighting for increased wages and more paddy were in no mood to listen to a man who was pontificating about a mysterious fish that should hunt for food and not be beguiled by an offered feast.

'What is being offered to us by the landlords – like the loans they grant us during marriages, like the arrack money they give us once a week, like the promise to provide us jobs when we join their association – these are baits. None of these will change our life. None of these will give us rights. None of these will make us own the land we till. None of these will make us their equals. None of these will make them treat us with respect. They are not waiting to become our brothers. They are using every opportunity to lure us into their fold. We should remain clever,' he said and, returning to his metaphor, added, 'and not bite the bait.'

Then he underlined the importance of sticking with the Communists because they were fighting for the rights of the workers and the tillers and the toilers. He also reminded the others that the Agricultural Labourers Trade Union was fifteen years old, but the Paddy Producers Association – an overnight mushroom – was only three years old. He believed this fifteen-year-old fledging movement would fight and uproot centuries of caste and feudalism.

'Oppression must be met with transgression,' he said.

So, he asked the people of Kilvenmani to be brave.

He also said, 'Transgression will be met with more oppression.'

And so, he asked the people of Kilvenmani to be more brave.

Dialogue 3: Karuppaiah swore that his pubic hair will not be plucked either by the elder-sister-fucking Gopalakrishna Naidu or the elder-sister-fucking god who created that elder-sister-fucker. The others might have nodded in vehement agreement, reaffirming their firm belief either in the tensile strength of his pubic hair, or in the epilatory ineptitude of Gopalakrishna Naidu and his maker.

Revolutions are usually verbose and, sometimes, they make too many promises.

Since the issue of funeral processions of the untouchables not being allowed to pass through the caste-Hindu streets had been raised at the meeting, a comrade took this opportunity to tell Kaveri and Kuppammal, the two old women who had the singular misfortune of standing next to him, '*Kilavi, kilavi*, when you both die, we will take your bodies through their streets.' And then, looking at Veerappan's daughter, who stood there mute and motionless, exorcism having failed her, he said, 'This is not only for the *kilavis*, but for you, too.'

He thought he was being nice.

The system of slavery in these parts has its own hate-list: late-comers, talk-backers, work-shirkers. This system of slavery believes in discipline and punishment and immediate enforcement. This system of slavery delivers justice faster than the local fisherwoman.

Now we take a look at a single case study.

Ratnam had been punished previously for one misdemeanour or the other, but even he was not prepared for the thrashing that he received on 18 December 1968, a date that would remain etched in his mind till his dying day. He was accused of having put the first signature to a memorandum against Gopalakrishna Naidu, he was accused of pasting the party posters in the Thevur market, he was accused of having beaten up the only man from Kilvenmani who had joined the Paddy Producers Association, he was accused of making his village rally around the red flag. He was called an ungrateful dog and a stupid pig and a whoreson's whoreson, among other appellations.

When a bleeding Ratnam goes to the Keevalur police station, Inspector Rajavel doesn't accept the complaint. He comes up with a convincing excuse – perhaps he says, 'This will work against you in the long run,' or he says, 'It is easy for me to file a complaint but that will turn both of you into permanent enemies,' or he says, 'You may be the secretary of the Communist Party in Kilvenmani, but do you have even a single person who would dare to give witness in your favour?' or one of those other things that policemen say when they have decided not to take you seriously.

A stubborn Ratnam is sent away home.

Today, at the meeting, he is Kilvenmani's hero. His first daughter, Virammal, married in Niruthanimangalam, has come with Sankar, her infant son, to see him. His fame has travelled far.

What did the party do? What could the party have done?

The party had seen glorious days. But the red salute could only unite up to a certain point. Fault-lines began to appear along the issue of untouchability. People started choosing convenient options that kept their caste codes intact.

Some deserted the party because the Indian National Congress made no ideological demands of them. Others deserted the party because the DMK had emerged as a new alternative to the Congress. Even the black-shirted Self-Respecters who did not contest elections started treating communism as though it were nothing more than a superstition. In East Tanjore, the party was patronized only by the Pallars and Paraiyars and other outcastes.

When approached by the people of Kilvenmani, the party made it clear that it did not make a decision on every isolated strike and uprising. It also said that it would not intercede with the landlords. The party said that it stood by the *cheri* because the *cheri* stood by the red flag. The party demanded loyalty: the feudal origins of this important trait were conveniently forgotten.

When they complained to the party about the 250 rupee fine that Gopalakrishna Naidu was demanding, the party told them not even to dream of paying up. The party said that soon Gopalakrishna Naidu's Paddy Producers Association would be banned, and therefore there was nothing to fear.

When the people said that the landlords would not give them work during the harvest season, the party promised to speak about the issue in the Legislative Assembly. The party said it had its representatives there.

When the party's local office told the party's high command that Gopalakrishna Naidu had held a meeting in Kilvenmani, the party's high command wrote back to the party's local office that the will of the working people would always defeat the feudal forces.

When the people found the theory too romantic to be reassuring and when they cried that Gopalakrishna Naidu had publicly announced a ten-day deadline for burning their village, the party's high command told them, through the proper channel, not to panic unduly. At this point, the party's secretary in Nagapattinam, Meenakshisundaram, reminded the perturbed villagers that he had written to the chief minister of the Madras presidency a few days before, pointing out all the havoc that was being wreaked by the Paddy Producers Association, and had sought for security for Kilvenmani. The high command unofficially said that the people would not come to any harm because their party was in a coalition with the DMK, the ruling party.

The party had morphed itself to enjoy the charms of the parliamentary system, and it consoled its cadre that it was playing by the rules of this new game.

But also to fulfil its role as a revolutionary force among

the proletariat for which it was originally intended, the party's local offices held public meetings everywhere. At Thevur and Tiruvarur. At Iluppur and Karuveli. At Avarani and Manjakkollai and Puducherry. At Sikkal too, where it had lost one of its most daring comrades.

The party continued to work among the people, the party continued to keep their spirits high. The party also provided protection.

The people remained silent, by order of the party.

In the midst of the struggle and the starvation, there are songs.

don't be blind, open your eyes; don't be meek, speak out; don't be a slave, straighten your spine. let the toiling blood thunder, let the crestfallen chest stand upright, let the working class unite! only our shackles shall be lost, in front of us is a golden world! the past is a dream, the future is a new epoch! these times are ours, comrades, we shall see a world of smiling faces and satisfied lives! long live the union, victory to the revolution!

These songs don't work in translation.

They are here only to remind the reader that the historical events of this novel did not take place in any English-speaking country. Don't you even try to get familiar with what goes on around here, for it is not only the sounds of my native land that you will find staggering.

Sorry.

This could be the first and last time you encounter many of the characters who have appeared in this chapter. I plead guilty to the charge of being ultra-utilitarian but, as far as I know, a novel is not about manners. You do not have to let people stay at your place only because it does not look nice if they are ordered out. Here, I simply push them off the page. Don't bother asking me about authorial decorum and all that jazz. I am not running for Miss Congeniality. I stopped practising politeness in tenth grade.

Because I have taken pleasure in the aggressive act of clobbering you with metafictive devices, I can hear some of you go: what happened to the rules of a novel?

They are hanging on my clothesline over there.

7. *A Walking Corpse*

My mother told me never to talk to strangers. Being a woman who has consistently disobeyed her mother, and having caused her a variety of near-fatal panic attacks and palpatations by having all kinds of affairs with all kinds of strangers, I take up this assignment with the belief that my mother will never come to hear of this trespass.

The job at hand goes beyond speaking/sleeping with a stranger; here, I am asked to share a blank page with Gopalakrishna Naidu.

Some day, I should sue myself for exposing a nice Tamil woman to sexual harassment and other untold dangers. Given my 'decent' upbringing and my mother's never-ending sermons on morality, I should have never stayed in a room with such a vile lecher, but fiction robs me of the little morality left in me. To be honest, I don't remember the door being left ajar, so I could not have walked out in the middle even if I had wanted to. Only the windows are wide open and, through the security bars, I send my apologies to my mother. Some day she will understand the multifarious circumstances that demanded me to step into the slippers of Seshappa Iyer, Gopalakrishna Naidu's legal consultant and Srinivasa Naidu, his regular letter-writer. Right now, I have a pressing, depressing job. I cannot allow my mother to judge me when I am at work.

As I am being briefed on the case – increasing Communist violence and intimidation through public meetings signal an imminent threat to Gopalakrishna Naidu, who will be reduced to a walking/sleeping corpse if the chief minister does not intervene – an unfamiliar letter pad is placed in front of me. When I am not set a word count, or there is no mention of a deadline, my imagination crumbles. Thankfully, he comes up with an instruction: 'All you have to write to the chief minister is that communism will kill me.'

I am unable to fill the gap, being a stranger to the grassroots situation. My memories of Marx are muddled, and the little that I have read of bootleg Charu Mazumdar seems to confirm this man's suspicions. I am perplexed. My heart swims in a restless sea of blood, and my speechlessness is a result of listening to this landlord asking me to prove that the Indian interpretation of a Communist dream of revolutionary reconstruction and reconstitution of society within the generous ambit of the system of parliamentary democracy poses a direct death threat to him.

'Yes, sir,' I say for his sake. 'The Communists could.'

He who has not dipped his hand in the blood of class enemies can hardly be called a Communist, sir. (The novel, being a non-assertive territory, allows me the privilege of an aside about an aside.)

'If you narrate the incidents, I can write them down, sir.'

I sound submissive enough for him to take the lead. He begins his haphazard dictation. I take notes. I fit them into the template of his former letters. Random paragraphs begin to appear almost as if they are revelations.

'I write this letter under grave and pressing circumstances requiring your urgent intervention. The Communists appear hell-bent on forcibly fomenting violence during the impending harvest season. Their leaders are in a mad zeal to outdo and outperform themselves and with this intention in their minds, they have thoroughly led the people astray. Nowhere else in the world have we seen leaders asking their workers to set fire to food grain when they know that it will cause them to go hungry. Why do they incite their workers to go on strike when they know that they will starve? They want the masses to be hungry so that they can direct their anger. The Communists clearly want to cause carnage during the harvest. There is sufficient reason to believe that they are planning a brazen attack on the landlords and, being the head of the Paddy Producers Association, I am their first enemy.

'In this particular instance, their immediate objective is to prevent the harvest through violence and bloodshed. They have decided to whip up frenzy in the district by holding a series of public meetings throughout Nagapattinam. Every day there are new posters that seek to provoke us. They put up these posters in order to pull us down. I wish to point out that there has been a procession before every public meeting. In each rally, they have chanted slogans against me and against our association. They have openly challenged me and openly threatened to finish me off. Within the last one month, they have held meetings at Thevur, Tiruvarur, Iluppur, Karuveli, Manjakkollai, Avarani, Sikkal and Puducherry. There are more to come.'

He reels off the dates. He names their state-level and local leaders: K. Balathandayutham, P. Jeevanantham, Manali Kandasamy, K.T.K. Thangamani, P. Ramamoorthy, N. Sankaraiah, M. Kalyanasundaram, G. Veeraiyyan, A.M. Gopu, Gnanasambandam, Dhanushkodi, Thandalai Kannappan, Paappakovil Kasthuriram, Sukumaran, Meenakshisundaram. Unencumbered by any guilt, I jot down details and remind myself that everything needs to be arranged in an alphabetical or chronological order. He continues to unload his rage.

'When the Communists are openly pursuing a path of violence, of what match is my non-violence, my *ahimsa*, my devotion to Gandhi? They have attacked my people, my relatives, my office-bearers. But I have stuck to non-violence. A week ago, when we organized a public meeting in the village of Kilvenmani on 15 December 1968, the Communists saw to it that none of the Harijan agricultural labourers from that village attended our meeting. Under duress and under misdirection, these illiterate coolies consider us their enemies and they consider the Communists as their fellow travellers and saviours.

'Communism teaches the people that we are their enemies. That is why we have stopped fighting against the Communists. Robbed of their only opportunity to create chaos, they feel cheated. That is why their anger is turned towards me today. They have issued death threats to me in their public meetings. Their posters celebrate my death; they publicly observe remembrance rituals for me. As a result of such mischievous Communist agitation, the labourers have become insubordinate and they have lost all sense of discipline. They absent themselves frequently from work, they go on strike at the slightest provocation, they use every pretext to demand higher wages – all these activities have caused catastrophic problems in cultivation. In the last two years, the lands have returned very poor yields, and unless the government takes strong measures to halt the Communist movement among the coolie labourers, production will register a further fall. Bearing in mind that near-famine conditions exist in a dozen districts, it is the first and foremost duty of the state to curtail the illegal activities of the Communists and crush them with an iron fist.'

I now work on a first-hand account of the indignity and humiliation that Gopalakrishna Naidu has suffered at the hands of the labourers. I am asked to write denigrating things about the agricultural workers: their brutishness, their blindness, their bad-assness. He plies me with stories.

'These incidents to insult and intimidate me are not isolated ones. There is a long history of Communist-incited violence in the Nagapattinam region. These agricultural coolies, most of them belonging to the untouchable communities, have been brainwashed into attacking the landlords. One must remember what happened to Congress leader Vedaratnam twenty years ago. Although he was an elected leader, he was attacked by more than a thousand people. They mercilessly removed his clothes and tried to parade him naked through the streets. He had to run into a nearby grove, shin up a tree and save his own neck from that mob. The police were helpless. The army took seven hours to traverse a few dozen miles because these Communists had felled trees and dug trenches. This was the fate of a Gandhian, a Congress leader, while the Communist Party functioned as an underground movement. Today, when they are left to flourish in the open, is there a limit to their excesses? The Communists imagine themselves to be warriors and revolutionaries, and they have trained the people not to be afraid of anything. Men who have been fattened on free food have no reason to fear jail.

'Is the police force protected against these violence-mongers? The police are routinely booed, hissed and pelted with stones. Being a member of the police force is no guarantee that they will escape the wrath of the Communists.'

I look at him in disbelief as he continues his dictation-narration-elaboration.

'Where lives of the *mirasdars* and their trustworthy employees are concerned, the Madras Police is no longer providing adequate protection. Only a couple of years ago, Venkatesa Iyer, the power agent of Ramanuja Naidu, was beheaded in full view of fifty people. This daylight murder took place right in the middle of a harvest. Every worker claimed that he was looking elsewhere – there was not a single witness for the old man's murder. Then it was decided at our meeting that there was no point in trusting the police. We started employing bodyguards. Even the governor's approval of a special police camp in our district has not solved our problem. The Malabar Special Police eat, sleep and march around town, but they are toothless tigers.'

Gopalakrishna Naidu sets about explaining his reasons for deploring police cowardice: 'On the ground, when we require security, they provide it. Not because they are strong; it is just their uniform. They are not powerful – I've seen policemen getting teased by *cheri* women. And they are certainly no match for the labourers who have been indoctrinated by the Communists to treat all *mirasdars* as enemies. Moreover, one of the earliest lessons of the comrades lies in teaching the farmhands to use their sickles and their sticks as weapons against us.'

Gopalakrishna Naidu, like the Kuomintang of China, shares the informed opinion that the peasant movement is a movement of riffraff. This prejudice alone is sufficient to elevate me to the position of an esteemed letter-drafter, as opposed to my Communist counterpart, who scribbles out complaints to provide for his next cup of tea and daily ration of cigarettes, or the 'writer' at the police station, who has to bargain for his bribe.

'Communism is actually a killer disease that has infested agriculture. It is worse than blight. Just like curtailing an unruly goat from causing damage to his crops, it is the duty of every farmer to take suitable preventive action against the Communists. This party is a curse upon the human race. It is the only party that seeks to divide us, set us one against another and make us enemies.

'This party is an imported poison – it is not from our soil, it is not meant for our people. It was brought to our shores by a man from Malaya, it was funded by the Soviet Union and, today, they have secret Chinese support. Their conspiracy is to keep India in the Stone Age. They target the uneducated section of society and make them oppose every new step that will take us towards development. This foreign evil is worse than the white man ruling over India.'

Every Communist gospel is deliberately reworked until it sounds as though it were a part of a sinister agenda to murder him. It sets him at ease.

This tirade continues until I interrupt him with a sentence that sounds like a doubt and is phrased like an apology. He shoos away my question like a fly.

We come back to the letter.

His command is straightforward: 'This letter should read like my suicide note.'

This is his working principle, his modus operandi, his craving to cash in on a sympathy wave. I catch the hint and decide to use every tear-jerking, heart-wrenching adjective at my disposal. Following his advice, I also learn to successfully imitate the formula of his previous letters and thus, under his guidance, I perfect my knowledge of officialese, petitionese and memorandumese. Five sentences ago, I came up with this one: 'The ongoing agricultural dispute relating to the aforesaid parties in connection with the determination of wage labour was communicated to the concerned officials in the above-mentioned letter and, subsequently, a copy of the same was sent to your esteemed office.' With practice, it becomes easier to draft this crescendo of nonsense on demand. I am now queen of clauses, poet of persuasive round-robin phrases. I swim in these sentences – here is a deadbeat one I want you to see: 'These immeasurable advantages are inevitable when such a protective mechanism is implemented for the benefit and the welfare of the farmers who strive hard to provide for the entire society. On behalf of the Paddy Producers Association, I request you to take into serious consideration the untold misery of the farmers and the everyday turmoil that they are made to face because of the violent activities of the Communists. I believe that the writ of your government goes beyond the mere matter of providing sanction and approval, and that your government will exhibit its autonomy by taking stringent action against those who disrupt law and order and destroy livelihoods.'

And so it goes.

We work under a ticking clock.

On the job, I learn that every single sentence needs to be revised until he expresses his unadulterated satisfaction. Evidence of his approval is a subject matter of intuition and jurisdiction, but it is mostly discerned when he bursts into an anecdote in the middle of my re-reading the middle of his sentence. The impulse to narrate, or to deviate, does not occur at the extremities.

My idea of the sentence-as-a-story collapses yet again. I tag along. He hunts for common intents and criminal intents and I accept each of his elaborate findings. He crams the letter with his fears and his facts. He fashions the letter to become history and historical intervention. He wants to include a reference to an incident ten years ago when he spent 200 rupees on the wedding of a farm labourer who was faithful to him. He wants to include another reference to a public meeting held last week in Kilvenmani in which he offered a truce to the villagers: jobs in lieu of joining his association. He wants to portray himself as a good man. I want to remain in his good books. I write my way out of this troublesome task.

Remember, dear reader, I write from a land where people wrap up newborn babies in clumsy rags and deck the dead in incredible finery. Unfortunately, I write for a man who cannot digest contradictions. His line of thinking often circles around its own grave, refusing to grow or develop into anything else. The Communists are evil, their peasant supporters are evil, Marx is evil, educated women like me are evil because they have read Marx. His thought processes have not expanded to understand dialectics; his wisdom is, instead, encapsulated in a handful of aphorisms he has heard growing up. The letter finally gets written with all these veritable inputs: childhood proverbs, random anecdotes, plagiarism of previous letters, standard petitioning jargon.

This missive to the state government ends with a misleading plea: 'Either you act now, or you shall never get the chance to act at all. Like Gandhi made the white man vacate India, there shall come a day when our nation shall be rid of these Communists, too. Your government can initiate the first step in this regard by taking necessary action to eradicate Communist violence from Nagapattinam, for which the entire agricultural community will remain eternally grateful to you. I also beseech your Honourable Self to take into account the grave threat to life that I face at present, as a result of which I have been reduced to a walking corpse. In these dire circumstances, I beg you to provide me with adequate security so that I can continue to discharge my duties as a farmer and lead people along the right path. The onerous and all-important task of annihilating the Communists lies in your hands, and I pray that you shall save society in this manner.'

I re-read the letter aloud. We rewrite sentences. We rearrange paragraphs. Sometime during the course of these corrections, a tight-lipped smile takes the place of his practised frown.

He compliments my patience.

Murthy, his agent, walks me to the door.

I have become the mouthpiece of a miserable man. Like ochre snakes that enjoy the smell of burning corpses, he is a sadist who takes perverse pleasure in seeing others suffer. These words that I have written down for him might one day come back to haunt me. They might be quoted word for word. They might be read and re-read. Action might be taken. Action might be spared. These words might some day save his skin. These words might some day speak for him, and in speaking for him reduce others to a charred silence. I cannot foresee all implications, all consequences. Right now, the letter seems to serve as a precautionary measure of protection. I have completed my assignment.

Now, what do I tell my she-has-a-knack-for-finding-out-everything mother? Will she not be ashamed of me? When she sits on the edge of my bed and strokes my hair and appears ready to lift the world on her shoulders, should I tell her that he winked at me? I think it would be wiser not to burden her with my stories. I should work it out for myself.

Was he not suggesting something when he said that crabs, like concubines, must be tasted on the sly? When he ran his hands along the barrel of his shotgun in short, smooth strokes, did he have sex on his mind? Since he was not a product of our poke-on-Facebook times and had, instead, made his earthly appearance as early as the eighteenth of November, one thousand nine hundred and twenty-four, was philandering with women a meritorious deed that asserted his masculinity? Did his rapes evoke immediate envy among other landlords?

Did his story scare me? Yes. Did he pull any tricks on me? None that I am aware of. Did we get drunk together? No, seeking a share of his scotch was not the politically correct thing to do. Did I send him consenting signals, as other women often blame me of doing? No. No. No. Reader, I have not married him. I was in the mood for some Dostoevsky that day, my mind was swinging with my mood and, reminding myself that men were despots by nature, I maintained an icy exterior, almost as if I was frozen by fear.

I had every reason to be afraid. He was a woe to women in five villages: Vandalur, Irukkai, Vadugachery, Thirukannangudi, Kilvenmani. People kept a tally of women he had raped, the virgins he had ordered to be sent to him, the girls who were never seen again. Because it was a shame that concerned them, because I was a visiting stranger from far away, because telling their stories would not undo the suffering, the women spoke in outlines, under condition of anonymity, buying into the belief that their trust would not be broken and hoping I would be spared the horrors they have had to face.

I was also cautioned by old men, who might have been excessively revolutionary in their youth, that merely uttering the name of this man would spread terror in forty other villages for thirty other reasons. I had everything on a tape-recorder somewhere, but that morning, the fear of upsetting him far outweighed the fear of him. Terror bred strange tales of extrajudicial deaths and summary disappearances and inquiry commissions and exhumations, so I chickened out, I wormed out, I went crawling to meet him.

Under these excruciating circumstances, I relied on reliable heresy to form my understanding of the man before I met him. I gathered some sure-as-stamp-paper facts. And a lot of stories. Sometimes the villagers went overboard, such as when they alleged that a goat was slaughtered for his every meal. The area of expertise of these villagers extended to all branches of storytelling. One villager described Gopalakrishna's house as being dark as a harlot's den of passion but, once inside, I found enough light to draft a memorandum-disguised-as-a-letter, drink coffee, carry on a filler conversation about his brown Alsatian and his red Plymouth and his ash-coloured Ambassador, and indulge in other such non-harlotic activities.

These narratives moved beyond biography to geography: an old woman at the village claimed that there are five ponds around Naidu's home but given my panic and tearing hurry on that afternoon, I never stopped to notice the kind of exacting details that are normally jotted down into iPads by wannabe novelists. I was also informed by this kind lady that the Pallars and Paraiyars and other lowered castes are not allowed to walk past the street where he lives. She suggested, unlike Google Maps, that in the interests of my own safety, I take a one-foot-wide, worn-out path that snakes around his backyard. Being a half-caste, quarter-caste, quarter-quarter-caste of dubious multi-casteness, I lost all opportunity for transgression when I was fetched to his home in his own ash-coloured Ambassador.

I had managed to get there without pissing him off straightaway. Sitting in the comfort of his home, I contemplated the stillness enveloping the rest of the locality and wondered if nobody in the neighbourhood stepped out for fear of offending him. Or, perhaps, there were other reasons. I will learn it all, learn it soon. (Such as his removal of hair, from everywhere.)

In the course of that afternoon, I allowed my roving eye to even size up this middle-aged man: white banian, white *veti*, the Singapore green belt, his loaded revolver, his thighs rubbing against each other as he walks around the room. His eyes, drunk on decadence, sized me up in turn.

Observation: He seldom smiles in the middle of work, but when he does, his rice-white teeth shine.

Direct Inference: He doesn't chew tobacco or betel-nut like any other vulgarly rich landlord-villain, who licks the corners of his mouth to titillate women.

Indirect Inference: He wants to present a clean image.

Observation: In that house of many, many rooms, he spoke as though he was revealing the secrets of the universe, and even a minute hint of distraction was sufficient to drive him into a murderous rage. His agent stayed still and silent all the time, but I cannot emulate his feat. Unable to cope at first, I later follow the cues of his Alsatian: watch him attentively, stay silent, nod at regular intervals, maintain a respectable distance.

Direct Inference: Gopalakrishna Naidu has not only an instinct for strategy, but also a love of spectacle. He is clamouring for an audience.

Indirect Inference: In spite of all appearances of intimacy, the relationship between the landlord and his agent resembles that of a mistress and her maid-servant.

Observation: Apart from his agent and me, the only other person in his home is the old man who cooks for him. Perhaps other people live there too, perhaps they all move about noiselessly. There is no real way of knowing because they are all silent. I listen carefully, I sometimes even miss his words, but I do not know what lies beyond our room in his low-ceilinged home.

Direct Inference: People keep away as a mark of respect.

Indirect Inference: I cannot be everywhere.

Lastly, it is vaguely comforting to realize that this entire exercise of milking every word dry, and mulling over the character of this man, has taken me only four hours and fifty-five minutes. In that short span of time, even as he supposedly sat in anticipation of death, Gopalakrishna Naidu has played the part of humble farmer to perfection.

part three

BATTLEGROUND

* * *

8. *Expression of Countenance*

It was Inspector Rajavel's turn to look at the dead and make a list. He inspected them head to toe and front to back, instructed the photographer to snap them from all angles, informed the doctors that they would only be allotted six hours to complete the post-mortem, and summoned up the courage to carry out the important task of filling out the inquest forms. He also took the precaution of surrounding himself with his favourite constables, those of the most pleasant disposition and, from time to time, he consulted the five-member village council who were given the onerous task of identifying the bodies. Though he was a genial man most of the year, he realized that the silent stares of the villagers aggravated his asthma, so he shooed them away. Quite naturally, he also developed a sudden aversion to dirge-singing, breast-beating old women.

If and when he were to rise in rank, he decided to re-design the standard templates that policemen had to fill out for every case of theft or suspicious death. Most of them required the repetition of the same sequence of events in three different formats, and a few of them, like the inquest form he was completing, posed rude, impertinent questions. It required him to list identification marks of the deceased, describe the corpse, closely observing all cavities (nose, ear, mouth, vagina and etc.) in good light during daytime, indicate the nature of the visible wound (incised, lacerated, bruised, fractured), look for ligature marks and signs of struggle, comment on the expression of countenance and the position of limbs, and report the presence of blood (liquid or clotted), saliva, froth, vomit or semen at the scene of crime. He was certain that the problem with these forms was not merely the absence of specificity, but also the thoughtlessness of generalization – perhaps a naive idiot had demanded the fingerprinting of every corpse that went to the coroner, but only a cold-blooded sadist could have come up with an instruction to the reporting police officer to note down the facial expression of a fire victim.

Although distracted by such disturbing thoughts, he managed to complete the work at hand, and went about looking after other procedures.

It would be cruel not to appreciate Inspector Rajavel's labours, and criminal to suppress the facts of the massacre. Therefore his observations have been shared hereunder, and the tabulation shall tell this tale.

1. Male, age not known, nobody can identify body; height 4'10"; marital status not known; protruding tongue, body totally burnt below the hip, hand flexed at the elbow, blackened blood all over the body
2. Subban Saambaan, aged about 70 years, son of Pakkirisamy; Harijan; height 5'; identification marks not visible as corpse completely burnt; married; hair partially singed, left arm and feet blackened, laceration on the abdomen
3. Kunjammal, aged about 30 years, wife of Thangavelu; Harijan; height 4'2"; extensive burns all over the body, skin on the right breast has peeled away; bloated corpse with lacerations and peeling skin
4. Poomayil, aged about 18 years, daughter of Kanchi; Harijan; height 3'11"; unmarried; hair partially singed; neck and left ear visibly burnt, charred hands and feet, legs blackened up to the hip, liquid-filled blisters all over the body
5. Jothi, aged about 10 years, daughter of Muniyan; Harijan; height 3'; not married; roughly three-fourths of her body has burnt with the exception of the left side of face and hair
6. Female, other details not known; height 5'1"; marital status not known; fragmented skull, visible female genitalia, body charred beyond identification

7. Female; height 4'8"; marital status not known; completely charred legs, teeth intact, visible genitalia and breasts
8. Female, name and other details not known; height 5'1"; marital status not known; head and the torso charred, legs have cooked away, visible female genitalia, absence of other personal effects
9. Female; height 1'2"; appears to be corpse of an infant; visible female genitalia; bones of the arms are seen, whole body is charred
10. Charred female torso; height about 4'; marital status unknown; completely burnt body, partially burnt female genitalia, unable to identify because of the extent of blackening
11. Charred female corpse; height 1'; appears to be an infant, body blackened beyond recognition
12. Charred female corpse, other details not known; approximate height 3'2"; marital status not known; severely mangled body, presence of breasts indicates body belonged to adult woman
13. Charred adult female corpse; height 4'6"; marital status not known; limbs completely burnt, visible female genitalia, fractured skull, other details not known

14. Name and sex not known, body charred beyond recognition; height 4'4"; marital status not known; burnt skeletal remains
15. Charred female corpse; height approximately 3'6"; marital status not known; appears to be a small child, a portion of the head has been burnt away, other details are not known
16. Charred adult female torso; height 5'; marital status not known; legs have been completely cooked and dismembered; presence of breasts and female genitalia
17. Charred adult female corpse; height 5'; marital status not known; body has been severely burnt, both the arms and one leg have complete burns revealing only skeleton; presence of breasts and visible female genitalia
18. Charred corpse of a female child; height 1'2"; marital status not known; one-inch long hair, legs are cooked and hanging apart, abdomen has burst, visible female genitalia
19. Charred female torso, presumably of an adult; height 4'10"; marital status not known; hair has been completely burnt, completely roasted below the hip, other identification not possible, presence of breasts
20. Charred corpse, sex not identifiable; height not known; marital status not known; only skeletal remains hang loosely as body completely burnt away

21. Sex unidentifiable from charred torso; height cannot be calculated; marital status not known; skull and skeleton remain, other details not known
22. Charred human torso; legs missing; other details not known
23. Charred corpse, sex not identifiable; height and marital status not known; only skull and skeleton are present
24. Blackened human corpse, sex not known; height 2'3"; marital status not known; completely burnt body
25. Charred female corpse; height 3'1"; other details not known; marital status not known; appears to be the body of a child, visible female genitalia
26. Charred male corpse; height 3'6"; marital status not known; body could be that of a child, skull has burst open, brain matter visible, other parts are blackened
27. Charred corpse of an adult; height 5'; marital status not known; skull intact, rest of the body has charred beyond identification
28. Charred human body; height 3'2"; marital status not known; extreme nature of burns make identification of sex impossible
29. Charred female child; 3'8" in height; marital status not known; female genitalia appears charred, body is burnt beyond identification

30. Charred human corpse; burnt to the bones making identification impossible
31. Charred female corpse; height 4'; marital status not known; female organs have suffered extreme burns, skull is intact, left hand has cooked away
32. Charred skeleton belonging to a human; other details not known
33. Severely burnt human body; height not known; marital status not known; skull separated from rest of skeleton, other details not known
34. Charred human corpse; skull and skeleton remain, other details not known
35. Completely charred female corpse; height 4'11"; marital status not known; no identification apart from visible female genitalia
36. Charred human corpse; only skull and skeletal remains are present
37. Burnt male corpse; presence of male genitalia; body has charred beyond identification
38. Charred skull and skeleton belonging to an adult human; age, sex, height not identifiable
39. Charred human corpse with only skull and bones; other details not known
40. Charred male corpse; height 5'4"; marital status not known; male genitalia burnt, appears to be an adult

41. Burnt, blackened, male torso; 3'6" in height; marital status unknown; skull and skeleton intact, male genitalia partially burnt, remaining body is roasted
42. A charred skull and tiny body; other details not known.

9. *A Minor Witness*

I was the first to come and tell everybody: Poomayil akka's appa was beaten up at the tea stall. I saw the fighting and ran away as fast as I could. When I was back home, I told them what I saw. All the men went there to help. Even Thaatha wanted to go and see what he could do. It would have taken him half a day to wobble all the way to the tea stall. So he was asked to stay. Even I was asked to stay. They asked us to look after the women and children.

Then the police vans came to our village. We knew that from the wailing sound of the sirens. My amma said the police only meant trouble for everybody. Seenu said the police had come there only to protect the *mirasdars*. She corrected him. That is what all the mothers do. She said that the police now wanted to catch our men, which is why the men of our village were not to be seen. They had run away. Only a few old men were left behind.

After having food, we came and sat in the open. The elders talked endlessly. They spoke of what had happened earlier in the day. They said the end was near. They also said this was not the end. They kept talking and it became dark and I fell asleep.

We heard whistles. They said rowdies were coming. Before I could see them, it started raining stones. We ducked our heads. We ran towards the edge of our street. Some of our men had come back in the dark and they began picking up bricks. Everyone joined in. Seeing them, I too began picking up stones. The men kept throwing stones. Natarajan started throwing the stones he had picked up. Guru joined him. I did not throw stones because my chittappa was watching. He could tell on me to my appa, who would believe his younger brother more than his son. So, I sat down quietly and watched the other boys act like men. Then we heard the gunshots. The old men ran into the fields. The women ran inside their homes.

Paappa akka, Ramayya maama's wife, was calling everyone to their house. Big with child, she walked with one hand on her stomach, afraid that it would fall off. She stood at the doorway and asked all of us to step inside. Vasuki was tugging at her sari, asking to be carried. Most of the women and children got inside.

Virammal akka, with her little son under one arm, pulled Guru and Natarajan into Paappa akka's house. She called them naughty monkeys. She told Natarajan that he was not even three feet tall and so he could not join the fighting. She told Guru that if he got out they would put a spear into him and he would never be able to see his sweetheart again. I was looking away all this time and she came to me. She asked me to run and fetch my sister and come back to her. She asked me not to go home. She asked me not to wander off. She asked me to come back in a blink.

I went to find my sister. I called her name.

I looked for her everywhere. I looked out until I could not see.

They were coming closer and closer. I stood there lost. Then Anjalai came and grabbed my hand from nowhere. We began to run. I could not go back to Paappa akka's home with her. Everybody was running there. I carried her and ran into the fields. We hid ourselves behind the crops, from where the dark night could be touched.

They started shooting. They were moving in. They were shouting. They set fire to the roof of the huts. They took the straw from one burning thatched roof to set fire to another. Then all the burning huts lit up the village. We saw fleeing figures. We heard bamboo splinters blast.

Then everything happened at once. We heard the screaming. The loud screams filled up the land. My little sister and I were crouching like monkeys. I held her tight to stop her running. She sat still. She did not know what was going on. I put my hand on her mouth so that she would not join the screaming. The screams stopped sometime later.

Then I came outside holding my sister. We ran towards our home. The sky was yellow and black with fire and smoke. I heard an old woman crying. When I got closer, I could make out that it was Maayi paati. She was with another woman. They were hiding behind a hut. They sat in such a way that only their faces could be seen above their knees. I understood they were without clothes. I took my father's lungis and gave them. They covered themselves. They came into our hut. We were all coughing. Maayi paati said that those who had come to attack us had gone away. So we went and sat outside.

A police van came again in the middle of the night. It went away after some time.

They did not come to us. We did not go to them. Maayi paati kept on crying. None of us could sleep.

The sun switched sides. Some men from our village came back with the light. The police tied them up.

Then the *thannikkaarar*, the watermen, came with their red lorries full of water. They said the fire could not be seen but things were still burning. We could not watch them work. We were not allowed near them.

From the policemen's chatter, I thought they were counting. I heard them say five, ten, twelve, twenty-five, thirty-eight. That many heads, they said. I was not sure. I don't know what happened after that.

We were taken away. I heard Appa was at the big hospital in Nagapattinam.

I did not know what happened to Chittappa.

I did not see the others.

10. *Mischief by Fire*

The streets are alight

and the marauding mob of landlords is at arm's length and those who have stayed behind in Kilvenmani apprehend its onward approach through shrill synchronized whistles piercing the cold night air and rapid gunshots being aimed at moving targets and the crackling noises of their homes bursting into flames and the screams of their women caught in the clutches of these attackers

and so they seek shelter in Paappa and Ramayya's hut because there is nowhere safer to go and because they believe in the strength and safety of their numbers and in staying together and so united they stand as they squeeze themselves inside and lock the door

and the mob soon arrives on its rampaging feet and tries to forcibly gain entrance and fails and in a fury sets the hut ablaze

and now escape involves the only available exit and the men by the door struggle to unlock it and they stumble out but they are hacked to death or pushed back inside

and in desperation a mother throws her one-year-old son out of the burning hut but the boy is caught by the leering mobsters and chopped into pieces and thrown back in and in that precise yet fleeting moment of loss and rage everyone realizes that they would die if their death meant saving a loved one and that they would die if their death meant staying together and that they would die anyway because it would not be as disastrous as living long enough to share this sight and so alone and together they prepare to resign themselves to the fact that they have mounted their collective funeral pyre

and the hut is fatally bolted for the final time from the outside by the mob leaving the dead the dying and the living dead in the crushed space to face the fire that is a merciless man-eating angry god who demands that everyone submits to suffering

and in no time at all the wails and the howls can be heard six villages away

but the cries are to no avail and in a matter of minutes the black smoke envelops them so they can no longer cry for help because their vocal cords have scorched and closed and suddenly inhalation itself is injury

and now the fire spreads with fondness and familiarity and the old men and the women and the children are bathed in blisters making touch their greatest trauma and long-ago tattoos of loved ones' names show up on their arms but they are almost already dead as they continue to burn and soon their blood begins to boil and ooze out of every pore sometimes tearing skin to force its way out in a hurry to feel fresh air and the blood begins to brown and then blacken

and at some point seeing becomes impossible because life has elapsed and so they no longer scare each other and instead they mourn in silence inside the torched hut as their muscles lose mass and begin to flex of their own free will arching joints into pyramids and the dying dance after their death as they are formed and deformed and their tongue-lolling soot-coated smiles only mean that pain is always followed by paralysis

and facial features disappear and flesh now starts splitting and shin bones show and hair singes with a strange smell and the flames hastily lick away at every last juicy bit as the bones learn to burst like dead wood and some of the singing bones spring to life and crack along the grain as if maintaining the beats of a secret and long-forgotten dirge because life has become extinct and there is no time for tears because death holds no terror

and so their lives go up in smoke but all of them are too dead to notice this vital fact of existence

and instead they burn all night fuelled by their own fat until the firemen come in the morning to wake them up by dousing their remains with cold water so that the police can pick up the pieces to match the mangled body parts and attempt an accurate headcount of the dead who have grown shorter in stature in one fiery night that left them as indistinct as roasted rats making individual identification impossible

and satisfy other official formalities like the flash photography from four different angles that shall record the coal-black colour of charred skin against calcined bones free of soft tissue and images of flesh hanging loose from corpses whose thighs end in abrupt stumps

and transport to the cremation grounds these fire-frozen dead with their fingers hooked into angry claws and the skin on their hands ready to come apart

and provide to the hungry press a picture-perfect portrait of a dead family where the cracks on the small child's skull resemble a spider's web and his brain spilling out is all pink and soft and squishy and nearby his mother kneels with another infant clutched to her breast in one tight embrace and it appears that all three of them have been stilled into this posture as if they were begging for life and look half-burnt as though the hasty fire stopped to show some mercy.

11. *In Police Custody*

It is not that night's incidents alone, madam, you see, this problem had been raging for three months and more, they were asking us to remove the flag, replace our red flag with their yellow flag, and you know this was not just polite please-do-it or can-you-do-it *panrengala? panna mudiyuma?* asking, they were threatening us *konnu poduvomda thevdiyamavaney*, we will kill you whoresons and then they were beating us up, I don't even want to go there, madam, and on top of that they started depriving us of jobs so there was nothing to do, nothing for the stomach and yes, this is how it went, so we went looking for work, it was not easy at all, this constant worry and fear but we were determined we would not be shaken up by these rowdies and as I was saying we would not give up the red flag under any circumstance you see because we had sworn to that effect and this *satthiya vaakku* was an issue of honour of our village and all the elders and all the little ones and everybody, man woman child, had agreed to this decision right under this banyan tree, *ingadhaan*, right here, right where we both are standing now, you see the village decided so there was no turning back and I'm not just saying that but we were ready to face anything, come what may and now you see, you see what has happened *ayyo ayyayyo*... what was I saying? Yes, we took the risk, what did we know then, would we expect this no no no this is not no not what we had in mind, we just knew that it was going to be quite a tough time really for us, no premonition that they would do exactly what they said they will do, burn Kilvenmani, anyway so for our safety everyone in our village would gather here, right here, daily at six or so in the evening, I could say after we had food and all and we took turns staying awake and feeling the pinch of black sky and it was sad, you know it had become a routine with us and it was like a village meeting, day after day we were hearing news of homes being burnt in other villages or news of girls being raped or somebody we knew being beaten up or killed *enneramum ithe pechuthaan* this was the only talk all the time... where was I? Yes, that day, that evening also the whole village had gathered and we were all tired like there was no tomorrow and talking of what happened in the afternoon and we were talking about the tractor that had come in from the south pulling a yellow-green trailer with a hundred, hundred and twenty, rowdy men really ruffian type rowdies you know the type who are used to just beating up people and yes these men got down and entered Muthusamy's tea stall, you know that one right? It's difficult to miss when you come here, it's the one that's right next to the barber's shop and where you would have seen all of us sitting on a normal day, anyway that's where the trouble started, these rowdies were there and one of the bastards Perumal Naidu from Irinjiyur, yes, Gopalakrishna Naidu's own village, picked a fight with Muniyan, you know him oh yes, madam, you were interviewing him earlier, he is our *thalaivar*, our village headman, yes, he's in the Communist Party also, everyone from here is in the party, see that is why it is important, this Perumal Naidu deliberately picks a fight with Muniyan because he knows this village will learn a lesson only when the leader is attacked and you see, how does he attack him, he says, hey, why are you standing so close to me? Get lost will you and our poor Muniyan he is fifty years old, he is the older generation you see, they have been used to so much bullying, he did not know what to do when a twenty-year-old boy talked to him in this filthy way, if it was me I would have hit that whoreson then and there and broken his jaw, but Muniyan is not that type, he is the type who will say, how can you come to my village and disrespect me like this, as if this politeness is going to work, and of course, they don't understand this nice polished talk, do they? No, they do not, in fact it only made them angrier… what was I going on about? Okay, back to the tea stall, this man Perumal was causing trouble and from what I heard he threw caste slurs around, insulted Muniyan and that fat pig Perumal, *avan summa pesikita irupaan*, he took a log of firewood and hit Muniyan, Muniyan was bleeding, and seeing that, Kanchi rushed to help and they hit him too then these rowdies beat up everyone in the tea stall, no one could say anything, or do anything, people are always stilled by sudden attacks aren't they, you will agree with me, and seeing that everyone there was mute the rowdies tied up two people, our people and took them to the landlord's place, the sun would have fallen and risen over our heads in the meanwhile, before we got to know about it, but *antha neram paarthu* that little boy, Nandan, had gone to the tea stall on an errand to buy betel leaves for his thaatha, so he saw what was going on *avanukku thalaiyum puriyala kaalum puriyala* he fled the place not being able to make head or tail of what was going on, and he came running, we asked him *ennada aachu* and he said he saw rowdies, our men being beaten, he was breathless *paavam chinna payyan*, we told him to stay back, we told four or five men to stay with the women and children to take care of them just in case some other trouble visited our village, *paarunga naanga apdi kavanama irundhom*, but all our precautions were going to be of no use, well, as I was saying, we had to go there as quickly as we could, we were all worried, at that time, we never knew what would be coming later that ill-fated day, *yaaru ninaichu paarthirupaanga*, at that time what mattered the most was running to the tea stall, we all went there, almost all of the men, we always move as one mass you see, it is for our safety, and there we saw our Muniyan and Muthusamy tied up, being dragged away, our blood was boiling, these two men were not just that or this, they were our village headman and party president, and their hands were tied behind their backs by those Naidu whoresons, *engalukku eppadi irukkum*, we were outraged, full of dread, we kept watching, they were taken to the landlord's house, even you can predict, madam, what would have happened, they were beaten up mercilessly, locked up in the chicken coop, all this was making my hair stand on end I don't even want to continue this, hmm, what to say, I was not the only one who was so angry, all of us were, there was still daylight left, and that's what the sun does, doesn't it, while there's light, there's a certain courage, so we went ahead to attack them, *cha* it's not only the light you know, have you watched people when they are returning from work, *oru veri irukkum*, there's this mood to fight, that's how it was with us, we were all tired and dried up and raw and we went right there banging his door, ready to face come what may, we were beaten up, blows rained on us, *semathiya adichaanuva*, we didn't take it lying down, we hit back bloody hard as we could, those whoresons were outnumbered, *adakki vaasichanunga*, and yes, we brought our Muniyan and Muthusamy with us through the back door, they were alive at least, that's what we thought, but you know, we felt that enough was enough with these sister-fuckers forgive my language, madam, we decided to file a complaint immediately, a complaint means we had to go to Thevur police station, we went there, there was no time to be spared, we were there asking them to come and catch the rowdies but the police would not shake their butts, you know what they were saying, your leaders are here, they are alive, nothing has happened to them, *ethukkuda thulrenga*, yes, those bastards had that audacity, they did nothing, they sent us back, you may not hear about these things in the city, amma, but here, the police are nothing but dogs, you would see that for yourself if you lived among us, I wish you came and wrote about them also, that's what I think, don't mistake me, one can fill a whole book with the atrocities done by the police, you should come again, oh yes, I understand, I know you are here to help, I will continue with my story, I was telling you about the police, what they did to us that day, no nothing, no action, after two hours some eight policemen turned up in their fancy screaming vans, those dogs did not come to the scene of crime, they did not go to the tea stall, they did not come to our homes, but those whoresons visited the criminal Ramanuja Naidu who had locked our leaders in a chicken coop, *avanukku moravaasal senjaanunga*, they never asked us if there was a problem, why we had filed a complaint or any routine duty that the police should do, they were sitting inside his house busy licking his ass, we were waiting outside, and look who comes there, Gopalakrishna Naidu's ash-coloured pleasure car pulls over, *kannum kaadhum vecha mathiriye ellaam nadakkuthu*, the sight of him meant something was going absolutely wrong but that was not the time for thinking, for me, when I saw that self-fellating whoreson I wanted to attack him, we were enraged, what stopped us was not fear, we stopped ourselves because we knew that if five of us killed him today he would kill fifty of us the following day, he is a ruthless fucker, sorry, but you know what I think now, if we had killed him then and there, such a big misfortune would not have befallen us, we missed that golden chance, and look what we got in return, you know there are times when you hear things but you don't believe it at all, that's how it was, Naidu was making a direct threat, telling the police he was going to burn Kilvenmani, he was going to attack the *cheri* if we continued our antics and he left and we dismissed it, it was not like he was doing it right then, right there, you know what I mean, to us it just looked like the day was drawing to a close, I think all this must have happened between six or seven at night and about eight or so, we were just waiting to get back and get some sleep, and did we sleep, did we even go to our homes, *enna nadandhuchu*, now the whole world knows, does it change anything, no, will it bring back our dead, no, sorry, I don't mean to upset you, you are only doing your job, sister, but you see that day dangles in front of my eyes all the time, I know it scene by scene, it is more clear to me than this moment, it is more real to me than the two of us here, talking, I feel as if all I need to do is to thrust my hand out and I will catch some mother-fucker from that mob, that's what I did that day, I'd never seen this whoreson before, he was one of the rowdies who had been sent to our village, he was asking us, 'which are the streets we should beat up, which are the streets we should burn', you see this mob did not know that we were the residents of the very village that they were heading to, when they saw the group of us returning from the caste-Hindu streets where the landlords lived they possibly thought we were another mob like them, sent to burn down the village, that's how random this bloodlust was, but because we were thirty of us we could act, so I caught the man who asked us this question and we dealt with them suitably, we were giving them a good fight, we were fierce, *oru veri, veriladhaan irundhom*, we were hitting back and holding them at bay, thankfully for us, the party had been contacted about the tea-stall incident by then, so when Thevur Kannan came there with our comrades from the nearby villages this mob ran away at the sight of him, but that was not the end of those devious sister-fuckers, you cannot imagine the levels to which they would stoop, there was one whoreson, may his dick be riddled with worms, he was talking with us, claiming that his name is Pandian, a fellow Communist, one of Thevur Kannan's men, but even as he talked he axed Sellamuthu with his billhook and then we realized that he is not from our party, that he is not Thevur Kannan's man, Kannan identified him as an agent from Irukkai, so we caught him and tied him up, we gave him what he deserved, *avan thola urichirukkanum aana neram illa*, and then we went back to our village, this night most of our men have gone away as usual to escape the police and it is just like any other *Margazhi* night, the cold winds are cruel and howl as they always do and we are all huddled together, even an old jute sack is a luxury in this month, our children sleep like mice with their heads inside old cardboard cartons so that the cold does not bite their little noses but this night they are hiding their faces in their mothers' saris, afraid of the stories that they have been hearing from us and only the older boys, by older I mean the ones who are wearing underwear, help us collect bricks and stones and that's how we arm ourselves because we are afraid that we might be attacked again and we, I mean the men, sister, we hide behind the coconut trees because we have spotted in the distance that the mob had regrouped, there were many, many of them now and they were coming back again and we know that first they have to climb over the bunds and then they have to cross the crops and so we were lying in wait and a hundred of them approached from all the four directions and they moved in step to the sound of whistles you see, that is how coordinated they were, and right at the beginning of the tar road they started shooting at us and we kept throwing our stones but it was simply no match for their guns, in fact our stone-throwing worked against us, you know, as every time a stone was thrown they used their torches to look for moving shadows and they too threw stones at us and many of us got hit, some ran away, some bled, some fell down, I remember that night clearly, in front of my eyes, Muniyan who is standing nearby throws a stone but a big brick lands on his head and from his body blood flows as if it were sweat and I don't know what to do, *kaiyyum odala kaalum odala*, I want to run away, I want to scream, but I stay, I hold him, I make him lean against a mud wall and then slowly I take him to safety, to shelter, to get a respite from the stones and the shooting and, in this snatch of silence on our side we hear them say, there is no one in this village, let us enter, and their mob enters and they start setting fire to the homes and in the light of these fires they see us leaving and they shout at us saying he's running away, he's running there and he's the man who killed two of our men and we don't know what to do and there is nothing for us to do and so we only throw stone upon futile stone at them but they have started to shoot at us and it is not simple shooting you see they have at least twenty-five guns with them, mostly local country-made shotguns not as good as the foreign guns but they could keep on firing, look at that coconut tree, it has the highest number of gunshot injuries, just like Palayam, they removed fifty-six pellets from his thigh at the hospital, and poor Veerappan had to lead him to safety down the mud paths in the dark and take him to Thevur and then to Keevalur and then straight to the hospital while we were ducking the gunshots coming our way and watching the mob remove the bamboo fences from our homes and as they advanced our people began to run away in fright, it was scary, seeing these men with their guns, and just then three black vans came around the corner and we felt the police had come, hope was there because our saviour was here, we ran towards the vans seeking help but Gopalakrishna Naidu and his henchmen stepped out of the vans and the trailers, *naanga ethirpaakave illa*, we were shocked, we were fooled, they burst into a brisk volley of commands: CATCH! STRIKE! HIT!, we were screaming, we started running for our lives we ran through the canals we ran through the ponds, *moochu vaanga neramilla ma*, we ran breathlessly, we had to save ourselves, we entered the fields full of paddy crops and hid ourselves there, and we were still, so still like we were stone-dead, we saw them set fire to our homes, we watched our village burn bright, we heard unceasing screams, we knew the worst was going on, but you see we could not go back, that would be useless, empty bravado, if you were there you too would have decided against going back, because if we went back we would be shot dead and we could not leave the fields because our shadows would give us away, we lay in wait and some time that night the police came again but they went back as if nothing had happened, they did not report any incident so we had to go to the police station and report the attack around midnight and the police came in their van at around two and by that time everything had been burnt down, I was crying that our people have been charred to death because the smell of burning hair was everywhere but no one listened to me, sister, so I decided to leave, I took Muniyan and Muthusamy away from Kilvenmani, it was panic, I was afraid that we might be attacked again that night, and you see, it is very important to save our leaders, they would have died for us, I made them board a *paara vandi* and sent them off to Nagapattinam, even I was injured, everything was going wrong at once, I was feeling forsaken, but I made up my mind and I went to the Keevalur police station and when I entered the station I saw Gopalakrishna Naidu come out wiping his filthy nose and *ennaala porukka mudiyala*, I started shouting *indha thaiyolidhaan enga sanaththa konaan*, he's the bloody mother-fucker who killed us all and the police restrained me by saying he is now under our custody, we can handle him, we can take care of the matter, and then they put me in a van to the hospital, that's how they deftly got rid of me, it looked like they were under orders to complete the crime by shielding the criminals, I was where I did not want to be, and here I saw something that will make any man shudder, my brother Palanivelu and my friend were carried inside like corpses and my brother's legs were hacked and both of them had at least forty injuries between them, it was atrocious, *indha aniya-yathukku oru alavae illa*, and this brutality happened because they had guns and we did not, these *mirasdars* had been allowed to have country shotguns and rifles and revolvers and pistols, complete with licence and all, but you know, sister, what the real tragedy is, not only were those barbaric whoresons allowed to have guns, but trust me, every single gun in the Nagapattinam taluk was deployed that night against us, we escaped only because we were hiding, we were not in the direct line of fire which would have killed at least fifty more of us, that's why we are breathing now, that's why we are undead, that's why I am able to tell you the story about that day, *kaalula neruppa kattikittu odanom, adhunaala thappichom*, we escaped because of our flaming feet, and at dawn most of us started returning to our village, you tell me, what else could we have done, even wordless creatures go looking for their dead, how could we stop ourselves, when we went we were promptly tied up to trees and beaten up by the police, *adhu mattuma*, they blamed us for the fires of the previous night and soon even the inspector general was here and he said this smelled like a village of corpses and he ordered for us to be untied and a police officer who had come with the IG caught hold of my friend Pandari Ramayya and accused him of the murder of Pakkirisami Pillai and Ramayya told him that it was true that he was caught up in a mob earlier in the day, that he was being attacked by the imported labourers who had come from Irukkai under their agent Pakkirisami Pillai, he said these labourers had been looking for trouble, and that he hit back only to defend himself, they were not convinced with anything he said, you see, he was a prize catch and they were in no mood to let him go, so they sent him to the highest official who was easiest to reach, so it was the district superintendent of the police force, *ennaala summava irukka mudiyum*, how could I let him go alone, so I went with my friend and there the DSP was in civil dress and he asked us to sit down but we said that we preferred standing and then he asked Ramayya – Tell me the truth, did you attack Pakkirisami Pillai – and he replied that there was a commotion and that most of the men from our village confronted the mob coming in the opposite direction with billhooks and knives and that we fought with them and that we were attacked by them and the DSP asked him to cut to the chase and come straight to the point and then Ramayya told him that it was *Margazhi*, the month of morning mist and the month of rain and slippery soil because of which he always carried a stick with him and that he hit this man with his stick because he was pretending to be one of us, but he was weaving his way in and out of our crowd and spearing our men at random and that he actually hit him only after he saw him stab Sellamuthu repeatedly with his billhook, and Ramayya said that it was what he did in the heat of the moment, he had not killed him, the man had only fallen into a nearby canal and then the others from our village had come hearing this noise and they saw this intruder and identified him as the agent from Irukkai, Pakkirisami Pillai, who imported the labourers, they tied him up and everything up to this was true, I say this because I was also there, I know that Ramayya did not have anything to do with that murder, but the DSP did not think so, when Ramayya was yet to even finish, the DSP left his chair, charged at him and slapped Ramayya as he kept repeating that it was true he attacked Pakkirisami Pillai for stabbing Sellamuthu, he had pushed him into the canal but he had not killed him but the DSP was in no mood to listen, instead he told his juniors that he should be thrown in jail and my friend was taken away, I was left alone, I made it back to the village and it was too crowded because everyone was there, the police and the newspaper people and the politicians, I managed to break the police cordon and saw them load the bodies into a lorry, half my village was dead now, those were my people, men who had roamed these fields carrying me on their shoulders, women who were sisters or daughters or mothers or aunts from whose hands I have had water to drink and food to eat, *ellarum uravu murai*, we were all related, I broke down, I was not even allowed to go near their bodies, they did not let me even look at them for the last time, I was beaten up by the police and taken into their custody, I was treated as a criminal though I lost everyone dear to me in one night, that's how everything worked you see, we had nothing nothing at all because we were fighting for everyday food but he had everything, he owned everything, those who burnt our homes were his slaves, those who were our landlords were also his slaves, the police were his slaves and even the politicians were his slaves because they had all eaten his salt.

I don't know what you feel, or whose side you are on but I have told my story, sister, I haven't lied to you, a man cannot lie when he has the taste of death on his tongue, I want you to write this all down and put it in the papers and tell the truth to the whole world. Let everyone read about what happened here and let them burn with anger. And yes, you can note this too, my name is Ramalingam, I live on the same street where the tragedy took place, I have studied up to the eighth standard.

12. *Some Humanitarian Gestures*

And since desperate times called for desperate measures, the extremely perturbed Inspector General of Police Mahadevan took certain liberties with his decisions. With the cosy benefit of hindsight, we could take shelter in blaming his haste but it must be borne in mind that on that particular day and under those pressing circumstances, Inspector General Mahadevan was left with no choice but to trust his instincts. When everything was in disorder, the atmosphere lent itself to rapid action. His first act was to get the suspects untied from the coconut trees which finally allowed the existing male survivors in Kilvenmani the freedom to be taken into proper police custody. His second act was to quickly dismiss the doctors who had been pressed into action at the behest of Inspector Rajavel. He ruled out a post-mortem or any procedure that involved taking the dead to a hospital. He reasoned that this was a modest humanitarian kindness that he could bestow on the victims. Nobody found the nerve to disagree, and the doctors were herded back to the hospital. Pleased that he had performed a gallant act of charity, he got the requisite courage to face his higher authorities.

Inspector Rajavel, in spite of his overwhelming deference to obedience, was unhappy with IG Mahadevan's decision to bid goodbye to the doctors. This country policeman had been proud of the huge team at his disposal and, naturally, he looked upon such downsizing as a personal affront. He was glad that at least the photographer, the firemen and the five-member village *panchayat* – made up of two untouchables (Thangavelu and Arumugam, a Paraiyar and Pallar), two Naidus and a Nadar for the neutrality – had been allowed to stay and identify the bodies.

Next, IG Mahadevan decided that the dead would not be returned to their relatives. This was his third charitable act of the day. He beamed with pride that he had solved the problem of handing over incomplete body parts of the unidentified victims. He was no longer rankled by questions: 'What if there was a mix-up of the dead children? What if husbands mourned for other men's wives? Would everybody at least get a complete corpse? What if the mass funeral fuelled a retaliation?' As he had anticipated, the Communists argued for the right of the relatives to perform the last rites of the dead, but he was clear that he would neither allow dismembered corpses to create confusion among the bereaved, nor allow the angry comrades to hold the state to ransom.

The Communists struggled to enter the village but the police cordon was rigid and impenetrable, and their leadership in Madras was mired in confusion and could not give them further orders on whether to break the *bandobust* or watch passively. Comrade Meenakshisundaram threatened direst repercussions against the police publicly, but used a local journalist friend to negotiate with them on his behalf, and as a consequence of his two-pronged approach, he and Comrade Sukumaran were let inside to meet IG Mahadevan. They exchanged pleasantries without any awkwardness despite being aware that the occasion was highly inappropriate. The Communists had a one-point demand: 'Give us our people', but the police chief was in no mood to oblige. He patiently cited law and order problems, medical formalities, historical precedents, legal obstacles and investigation procedures, but to no avail. Clearly, such cold logic and persuasive techniques did not find favour with the Communist leaders, who stuck to their stand.

'I know you know this but do you think it is my personal decision? As a police officer, I want to let you know that we have been given shooting orders. How can anybody guarantee that their funerals would be peaceful? Who can assure us that there will not be another blood bath?' IG Mahadevan said.

'But the bodies belong to us.'

IG Mahadevan stayed silent for a long time. 'I don't disagree,' he said and, pointing towards the burnt hut, remarked that it was easier to pluck hair off a hen's egg than to find matching pairs of legs, arms, a torso and a head for each of the dead from the heap of corpses.

'No hands. No legs. No names. That's our problem. Our people were murdered, and we need their bodies. They died defending our red flag and they will be buried under our red flag. Give them to us,' Sukumaran demanded.

IG Mahadevan did not relent. 'They might be dead meat, but we cannot ration them, *comrade*,' he said.

Before he could retort, Comrade Sukumaran was escorted away. Comrade Meenakshisundaram followed him out, shouting anti-police slogans.

Born without eyes, the fire had used its feet to move. Lacking the forgiveness of water, it had burnt them with blindness and bitterness. So, that morning, the *cheri* did not carry the roses-and-marigolds smell of death. Only the coppery sick-sweet smell of charred flesh: a smell like nothing else, a smell that was almost a taste, a smell that was meant to be smuggled to the grave. Through the smoke clouds that hung heavier than mist, the police van returned to Kilvenmani to fetch the dead. The living had been taken away to the hospital, or taken into custody. Subban was the first to be loaded in, followed by ten-year-old Jothi. The gravedigger and his granddaughter. Kunjammal and Poomayil, wife and sister of Thangavelu, the only two others who were identified. Then, as if out of deference, the dead mother cradling the dead child. Then the men and the women and the children and the disjointed limbs and torsos and legs that were stumps and standalone skulls and unclassifiable chunks of charred flesh. Stick men and stick women and stick children: dark and devoured by fire. The remains of two babies muddled into a mess, so they were not on the list of the dead. Such death diminished the pain of procedure. There was no time wasted applying the rule of nines, no necessity to extract dying declarations.

Inspector Rajavel was worried about the business of death certificates: should he get one made out for every dead body? How could those certificates carry names when only four corpses had been identified? Should they be numbered instead? The official count of the dead stood at forty-two. (The other two dead were habeas corpses. The police did not account for their deaths. Sankar: a one-year-old baby whose mother had thrown him outside the burning hut in the belief that he would be left to live but was caught by a gunman on his rifle bayonet, hacked into pieces and fed to the fire. Less spectacularly, a baby girl who had burned, leaving behind no distinct trace.)

Destination of the dead: Paappaan Sudukaadu, Nagapattinam. A cremation ground named after Brahmins but used for untouchables. The police van, meant for paved roads, takes the forty-two (plus two, silent) corpses through the main roads, through the caste-Hindu roads, through the banned roads, through the debarred roads. Having accompanied them on their final ride, Inspector Rajavel supervises the burning. In one common pyre, the bodies are piled one on top of another: as haphazard as they had been found, as haphazard as firewood. The cremation ground is infected with sufficient police presence to keep away the Communists who might launch a strike, retaliate and seize the bodies. None of the relatives is allowed to the funeral, not even the fourteen men with gunshot injuries who are held in custody at the government hospital, who refuse to eat unless they are allowed to visit the dead. Local villagers are roughed up. Schoolchildren turn up to have one last look at the dead but they do not leave.

The cremation is no electric-powered paradise. The charcoal-like corpses are set alight. The firewood is not sufficient and, in a final act of defiance, the bodies refuse to burn. Inspector Rajavel is angry with the disobedient, stubborn corpses. He calls up the district collector, gets his permission to buy and bring in another load of firewood. The fresh supply of fuel and the efficiency of kerosene ensure that the dead disappear into ashes.

With the air of a man who has charmed a dead snake, Inspector Rajavel prepares to prepare a catalogue of remains that will constitute evidence.

All that is left are a few bones. His efforts, however, have enabled him to be in possession of red paper shells, cartridge covers, shot-wads: signs of a shooting spree. Charred bamboo splinters represent a ghostly village of missing roofs, gutted mud-walled huts and half-burnt homes where only the grinding stone has withstood the fury of fire. A collection of pots and pans too, almost as if they were the remnants of a long-ago civilization.

And there is the seized material from the suspects: a Webley & Scott, a Stevens Arms Company firearm with 12-bore single barrel breech-loading capacity and other, country-made shotguns.

A pile of paperwork awaits him. To link the crime with the guns, these suspect firearms have to be sent to the forensic laboratories. There is work with the doctors, work with the reporters.

He meets with Jameson – proprietor and photographer of the Eastern Studios – the man called in to capture this Christmas Day massacre. Like a Buddha in the backyard, the photographer has provided still-life renderings of destruction: thirty-five burnt huts, forty-something charred bodies heaped in mounds, dust that clouds the landscape. Inspector Rajavel refrains from looking at the pictures of the victims. In these hard times, he derives strength from facts and figures bonded by facts and figures, not photographs that flicker like ghosts.

Constable Muthupandi has brought in the measurements of Ramayya's hut: the courtyard was seven feet by eleven feet, it led into a front room eleven feet long and an inside room that was eight feet long and nine feet wide. The walls were five feet and six inches tall. The roof has been completely burnt, the door and its frame have been charred, but the monkey door-bolt has stayed intact. From the inside room, the policemen have collected pieces of singed clothes. Then, Constable Nayagan lays out the metallic remains: two toe-rings, a talisman, and a silver fig leaf that covered some child's shame.

Everything is carefully sealed in a bag.

Every one of them knows that evidence will never be enough.

part four

BURIAL GROUND

* * *

13. *A Survival Guide*

Everything would die its natural death. The visit of the politicians would fade out and journalists would stop being eager and this news would disappear from the headlines and fact-finding missions would be bored of report writing, and life in Kilvenmani would moodily limp back to normal. Even the men in uniform would stop being bothered. But, for the time being, that is all in the future. The men who have survived are nursing their wounds in the hospital, or in hiding, or huddling in jail. Every man in Kilvenmani over the age of seventeen has a case slapped on him. Back to work, the police are doing their duty. Most of the men are implicated in the Pakkirisami Pillai single murder case; the police, in love with variety, generously give everyone multiple sections of the Indian Penal Code.

Life, weighed down by death, weary of destruction, goes on.

So many women of the village have been wiped out, there is no one to sing the dirges of death. Men are not allowed to see their loved ones' corpses; they take their mothers sisters wives daughters sons for dead because they have not been seen since that night. They secretly hope someone survived, they pray that those presumed dead send word. When someone appears after staying two days in a stranger's house in another village, Kilvenmani erupts in joy.

People are worried that those escaping death might have been captured alive. They think of Comrade Chinnapillai whose body has never been found, they remember their young women who were kidnapped and carried away and raped and killed and buried in some coconut grove. Until everyone alive turns up, the list of dead is not confirmed.

They are outraged by these inconceivable deaths: the young did not deserve to die and the old left them without any warning. Now burdened with mourning, it is beyond the means of the living to try and make meaning out of the randomness of death.

Remember that there lived, once-upon-a-time, in-a-tiny-village, an Old Woman who made her debut in the very beginning of this novel? You were promised that if you were patient enough, you would hear her speak and watch her move through these pages. Now, it's time for you to know her on a first-name basis. Meet Maayi. Before you make up your mind as to whether you want to greet her by shaking hands or falling at her feet or doing a combination of the above that takes into account your combined cultural sensitivies, remember that she is a busy woman. Once married to the village's witch doctor, it has now fallen upon her to hold her people together.

Before we rewrite history and relegate her man to the margins, a word about him. In the tiny villages where he was known, a certain religious hysteria surfaced whenever his name was mentioned.

It began when he tamed a notorious, anklet-wearing vampire. It was rumoured that this bloodsucker walked backwards and that those who saw the fire burn in her eye sockets dropped dead. But he had convinced her to go away. He had made the meanest ghouls promise him that they would move to other graveyards. He offered arrack to angry spirits. He sorted out every squabble between husbands and wives, brothers and cousins, shopkeepers and neighbours. Mute children, left at his doorstep by dejected parents, returned home talkative brats. Men went straight to him when they fumbled and failed their wives night after night. Possessed women were brought to him to have their devils driven away. He gave them sacred ash, healing their frenzy with nothing but neem leaves and his honest eyes. It worked as effectively as his peacock oil concoction for epilepsy.

The people of Kilvenmani would always touch his feet and ask for his blessing. They loved him for the comfort with which they could share their secrets. The gods spoke through him and the demons listened to him and there was nothing more any man could ask for. This man, with the matted hair, was the soothsayer and the spell-maker.

Sannasi could have brought solace to this bereaved village if he had not been murdered three years before.

The strangeness in Letchumi's head never subsided. She had become so dizzy that police battalions and hired rowdies and armed landlords kept running away as flag-bearing Communists and the dead chased them through her, ear to ear, in unceasing waves.

One day, when Maayi came to her carrying food, since she had not eaten in days, she took the old woman's hands and put them on her forehead, on her eyelids, at the base of her throat and told her that she could feel a hundred fights inside her body and nobody retired to take rest and their madness made her fly. Sometimes they made her hurt herself. She also told Maayi that she thought her dead mother, Kaveri, was inside her, that her dead friends, Virammal and Sethu, were inside her and that their hearts were beating in her breast. She was sure that their bodies had been burnt, but their souls had escaped to safety and now they were alive within her and soon they would begin to speak. Her complaints varied, but the relentless throbbing never stopped. The dead were devouring her from the inside. Again and again, she collapsed in the chaos.

When Muthusamy saw the state of his sister, he broke down. Maayi told him that Letchumi was not alone. Everyone in Kilvenmani carried the ghosts of their dead.

In that village of overnight widowers, Muni's sorrows never cease. His family has been virtually wiped out. He has lost his father and mother, he has lost his wife and two daughters. And he has lost two sisters-in-law, three nephews and a niece. Eleven members, a quarter of Kilvenmani's dead. Muni's father had been the village gravedigger, so death held no novelty. What has happened now was not in the realm of death, it went way beyond.

His infant son, Paneer, who was still suckling, is now motherless. His first son, Selvaraj, whom he had given in adoption to his own parents, is also an orphan. His elder brother, Ratinasamy, lost his wife and all their children. His younger brother, Seppan, lost his wife and little son. He and his two brothers are now orphans. No family, only the three brothers sticking to each other for solace.

Every evening, they drown their sorrows with drink.

Arumugam is afraid for his daughter. Asked to identify the dead, he points out Jothi, her classmate. That is when the dread enters him.

He cannot move, but he will not let his little girl out of sight. She is caught between his fear and her lack of any idea of what happened. The terror talks to her body in strange ways. She shivers when she is alone. She has seizures in her sleep. She needs to be held by someone. She needs that smell of armpits to soothe her, breasts to rest her head on. She keeps asking about the others, her friends. She calls them all, one by one. They are dead, but to her it doesn't matter. Perhaps they come and stand in a line. Or perhaps they hold each other's hands and form a neat circle. Perhaps they clap their hands for her. Perhaps they dance too, one leg in the air, half-bent, and then the other. Perhaps they can only stay still. She doesn't tell the elders about her friends. After she's called their names, after she is sure that all the boys and the girls have come, after she has finished playing, she spins like a top under a frenzied whip, and falls down in a swoon.

That is when Maayi is summoned.

Maayi thinks the men who were wounded by the guns are lucky. The men who were beaten up too. The men who were hurt, then the men who work in the party, then the men who are friends of the men who were hurt and who work in the party and thus, almost everyone is lucky. Their pain grounds them, prevents them from hurtling down into other worlds, from disappearing into the abyss.

Pain. And anger.

Anger prevents Kilvenmani from disorienting itself. Maayi sees how the anger keeps the people together, injects them with life, provides them a reason to live, pushes them into action. Sometimes, the rage borders on madness. She can see it everywhere, just as she can see the sorrow and the sudden emptiness. She does not want that rage to turn inwards. She does not want the sorrow to eat up the men and the women and the teenagers and the children. She is afraid for her people. The full-hands, the three-quarter-hands, the half-hands and the quarter-hands. Every one of them.

Everyone.

The ochre sparrows are on fire. The pigeons in white flight are on fire. The sun is on fire. The clouds are burning at the edges. The flaming yellow of the moon is on fire. The stars pour with sparks that will scorch the earth on touchdown. The gold of the paddy fields is on fire. The burning brown mounds of grain and mountains of hay are on fire. The red flag at noon is on fire. The gutted huts have roofs of fire. The ponds are bright and burning as they splice up the sunlight. The roads catch fire whenever a stray vehicle kicks up dust. The sand is speckled with fire sparkles. The gods have blackened into death and the camphor only lights up their charred corpses. Women carelessly wind the fire around their hips and across their breasts. Girls carry fire in the ends of their curling hair and they pretend not to notice at all. Men swallow the fire as if their stomachs were stoves. Children catch fire when they run because the wind shaves their skin and sets them alight. The air is full of golden fire-dust. Everything is ablaze. Everyone is glowing. He cannot save any of them but he screams all the time. He shouts at them to stop. No one pays heed. No one stops to douse the fire. Everyone is hurtling towards death and Veerappan can only watch them burn away like his red towel.

The mornings passed without incident because there was work. Thangamma had to survive for the sake of the village. She had to go to the hospital to look after her husband. Whenever a journalist sauntered into Kilvenmani, she joined the others and spoke about what happened and how she felt. She told them how she saved her mother-in-law, Araayi, that night. She described how she led her little children, Shenbagavalli and Mani, to safety by herding them to the nearby school. She spoke of Kerosene Govinda pulling at her clothes and how she fought back fiercely. *Why are you running away, you whore?* She repeated his words verbatim.

She never cried so they listened to her and asked her more questions with the hope that she would start weeping and they could go back with a story of how strong women crumbled.

She never cried in front of them.

Tough during the day, Muniyan's wife allowed the nights to torment her. She could not stay there. She walked wherever her legs carried her. She returned by daylight to her home. She wanted to be moving in the darkness. She wanted to be alone with her sadness.

Tongues would wag in any other village. Here, the men were too broken to notice and the women were too scared to follow her on her nightly walks.

Living the nightmare, she had wandered very far away from the land of sleep.

She was in no mood to turn around.

He refused to talk. Death had driven a dagger through him, muting him.

His mind went in impossible loops: weeping people made the dogs go crazy, visiting journalists made the people weep. Politicians planned these fires, police obeyed the politicians, landlords controlled police battalions, women who were forced to sleep with the landlords did not murder them and that is why these tragedies happened.

With his voice trapped in his head and his words stuck in stranger corners, his memory healed, his memory hurt, his memory turned against itself.

On the sixteenth day, when the mourning village fed its dead ancestors, placated their tormented souls and told them to rest in peace, Karuppaiah's memory seized him at a weak moment and drove him to take away the only life he had.

She would not allow a stitch of cloth to cover her body. She lay naked on the mat, through the day and through the night. She threw away all her clothes. When Maayi forced her to cover her shame with an inskirt, she tore it off. She was coherent when she talked about the Communist Party, but she refused to talk about her hatred for clothes. Maayi confined her to their hut.

She waits for her to recover.

Caught by the hair, pushed to the ground, stripped naked, beaten up. Scars on her left cheek, a sickle split on the right side of her hip, red welts on her palm from fighting the men. Maayi, as Packiam's mother-in-law, knows that night too well to wonder what went wrong.

Periyaan went about his work as usual. He was there at his son's tea stall. He was there at the party office. He was there at the hospital. He was there, where he was required to be. But in the nights, when he was drunk on arrack, he would begin to scream. Gopalakrishna Naidu, come here and get fucked. Either this, or other colourful, powerful variations. Gopalakrishna Naidu, if you are a man and if you have balls, come here and get fucked. Gopalakrishna Naidu, if you are born of one father, come here and get fucked. Gopalakrishna Naidu, if you are not the son of a guest, come here and get fucked. Gopalakrishna Naidu, if you have not slept with your mother, come here and get fucked. Gopalakrishna Naidu, if you are not busy fucking your sister, come here and get fucked.

The screaming went on, all night long.

Come here. Get fucked. Come here. Get fucked.

Everyone agrees that no one deserved to die. Everyone believes that they should have been dead instead...

Instead of Muthusamy's mother, Kaveri, who had gone away to her mother's village, but had rushed back to Kilvenmani when she heard news of her son being beaten up by the landlords.

Instead of Thangavelu's wife, Kunjammal, who had broken the news of her pregnancy to him only that morning. After her three-month-old daughter had died, Kunjammal, as if to punish herself, had not slept with her husband for three years afterwards, and now never would again.

Instead of Ratnam's daughter, Virammal – with a one-year-old son – who had fought with her mother-in-law and husband to go to Kilvenmani to see her father and stay with her little brothers for a week.

And everyone wanted to be dead instead of Ramayya's wife, Paappa. Nine months pregnant and expecting a baby any moment, she had kept calling them all to safety, she had offered everyone her hut for refuge.

Maayi alone sensed his mutinous intent. When she touched his hands, she knew how he spent his day. The dirt under his fingernails told her where he had been. She would have bathed him then and there – he was only a ten-year-old child. But she did nothing. She knew the boys who wanted to be treated like men and the men who wanted to be treated like boys. If it had been her grandson, she would have taken him on to her lap, rubbed his tiny toes, and told him that he could not do anything. Nandan was not like any of them.

Maayi was aware of the anger that stiffened this boy's hands. She knew the knots behind his nerves, the bones burning in his knees. He had been throwing stones. *Onnu. Rendu. Moonu. Naalu.* He had been breaking things. *Naapatthi-Onnu. Naapatthi-Rendu. Naapatthi-Moonu. Naapatthi-Naalu.* He had been keeping count. He had not forgotten what he had seen.

Taking his restless hands in hers, she tells him to send his anger to his heart, to his head. If you keep it in your knuckles or in your fists, it will slip away from you in a blink. Even if you watch it all the time, it will vanish.

You have a big man's anger, she tells him. You need an old man's patience.

In the days following the tragedy, Maayi managed to keep a grip on her own sanity.

The journalists who come there seek her out. They want her old-woman ways, her old-woman words. They want her version of the story. The photographers treasure her – she without a blouse, she with the long dangling earlobes, she with tattoos all over her arms. They delight in her postures: how she sits like a bird about to launch into flight, how she spits tobacco as she speaks, how her hair comes loose when she sings a dirge, how her hands lift in the air to shape the desolation of the entire village. They watch her fling sand into the skies and slap her thighs as she curses the landlords. They capture her eyes when she bids the flowers of the graveyard to grow in the homes of the murderers.

The living in Kilvenmani lack life. Everyone is something else: there are the ones who do not eat, the ones who do not talk, the ones who do not bathe, the ones who do not step outside their homes, the ones who do not step inside their homes. It is strange, the way in which the village has exchanged its sorrow for insanity. She sees everything as if these are ordinary things. As if she has seen greater horrors. But she doesn't tell their stories to the journalists. These stories are her village's wounds of shame, they cannot be displayed to passing spectators.

Maayi heals the living.

Maayi also hears the dead.

On new moon nights, they sing the dirges of their death. In the silence of their lament, she senses that they have stolen her words.

14. *What Happened Afterwards*

They came with relief supplies, we shouted them away. Could they produce our dead back again, in flesh and blood? Could they give us back our wives and our children and our parents? What were we to do with their clothes and their utensils and their rations? Were suckling infants underground comrades? Were schoolchildren full-timer Communists giving speeches from big, public platforms? Was forty-four lives the price for an extra measure of paddy? Was this our sacrifice for staying with the red flag? Why were our people in jails when it was we who had died? Were they running a state or a slaughterhouse?

We told them that we did not want that blood-soaked, flesh-smoked rice.

We told them that we did not want compensation, we wanted justice.

They shook their heads and shrugged their shoulders and walked away.

*

Three days after the tragedy, Comrade P. Ramamoorthy, our party's state secretary, came to the village. He came from Kochi, where he had been attending the party's eighth congress. Communist leaders from neighbouring districts came, leaders from other parties were also here.

We knew that politicians would never skip an important death. If they could not be at the spot of death, they would come to the funeral. If they could not come to the funeral, they would come to the sixteenth-day ceremony. If they could not come to the sixteenth-day ceremony, they would come any day. *Thukkam visarikka varuvaanga.* They would come to enquire about our sorrow. How big it was, how deep it was, what were its dimensions, what was the death count? They wanted to know everything so that they could feel bad for the bereaved. We would cry and they would wipe away our tears. They would cry and we would tell them not to cry.

Karunanidhi, the man who was going to be the next chief minister, came to our village soon after the tragedy. He was from these parts, although he had left for the city to make it in politics. When he came and met us, the police and newspaper people followed him around. After the sorrow-questioning and sorrow-hearing, he said things that would give us strength. He swore his loyalty to us. He said he would make us an offer we could not refuse.

He asked all of us to move to Thirukkuvalai to be under his protection. He said we would be safe. He said he would give us land and schools and homes. We listened to him. We understood his good intentions.

The next day the papers carried this story. They carried it along with a picture of Maayi weeping as he spoke to her. She came running to Muthusamy's tea stall to see the picture. And she said, 'Even if all of us are going to die, we will die in Kilvenmani itself.' Everyone agreed.

*

Everything hinged on the first complaint that we had given at the Keevalur police station. This had had to be any one of us – the one whose leg was operated upon, the one who got fifty-six pellets of birdshot, the one who lost eleven family members – and it was Jayabalan, because he had rushed to the police station that night itself.

The complaint read: 'I am Jayabalan, son of Ayyavu, Hindu, aged about 30 years. I live in Pallaththeru in Kilvenmani. At about 10 p.m. tonight, Gopalakrishna Naidu and 20 or 30 men came to our village from Irinjiyur. They entered our street Pallaththeru, and set fire to my house and shot at me. I have sustained gunshot injuries on my neck and face. They also set fire to other homes. I don't know what happened to those inside the homes. Kathamuthu, the teacher at Melvenmani, brought me on his cycle to Keevalur. I asked this to be read out to me and it is as I said.'

It was as he said.

We were the complainants; our village, the wailing child.

Later this complaint would grow a pair of hands and a pair of legs and a dark face with only eyes on it and become our legal case. The police would half-heartedly appear to fight to prove this true.

The fate of our village went into strange hands, strange lands.

*

While our village burned and smouldered, Annadurai, the short-statured, soft-spoken chief minister lay on his death-bed, looking forward to the fanfare of his funeral the following February, which fifteen million people would attend. News had reached his office at Fort St. George, as it was meant to. He summoned up some energy and he said: 'This incident is so savage and sadistic that words falter and fail to express my agony and anguish.'

And when asked for more, he added, craning his neck: 'People should forget this as they forget a feverish nightmare or a flash of lightning.'

Everybody quoted him again and again: the newspapers and the radio and his partymen. Everybody revelled in the poetry of his flash-of-lightning expression. They marvelled at his unceasingly alliterative powers.

We were forgotten. That was all. This was it.

*

We think the problem with the politicians is that they have seen too many deaths. To them every death is only a funeral. Nothing more, nothing less. Or every death is like a marriage, or it is like a meeting, or it is like a procession. If they don't have to make a speech at a death, some of them are relieved and some of them are offended.

We knew that everyone came to our village because of death. We knew this because they never came when we struggled or when we starved or when we silently waited for death. The death was the climax. The death was like the moment in the movies that no one wanted to miss and where everyone cried.

In the movies, everyone soon goes back to whistling. We don't know what happened after they came here and cried. We never found out.

*

There were messages of condolence every day. Periyar EVR, the great old man that he was, condemned the massacre when he came out of hospital two days after our tragedy. Everybody was waiting for what he had to say. He said it was time Indian democracy was destroyed. He said Indian people were barbarians. He said that after the white man left, the country went into the hands of charlatans. At ninety years of age, he had not seen anything so full of gore. He compared this incident to the assassination of Gandhi.

He spoke about the forty-two (plus two, silent) men and women and children who were burnt to death. He said that politicians committed this atrocity in broad daylight.

He said that such acts took place because capitalism prevented the creation of laws to hand down stringent punishment to criminals. He also said that there could be no hope for justice in a land where ninety out of a hundred judges were revengeful, casteist and selfish. He said corruption was ruining this country.

He was angry and he showed it. There was little else that could be done when the government was actually run by his protégé. In his hopelessness, he foresaw our fate.

*

The future had been tied to the past, so we heard our history over and over and over again. We always ended up hearing this history wherever we started. Some days it was about the curse of capitalism. Some days it was about the scourge of feudalism and how it had to be fought with force. Some days it was about caste, but only at the edges, at the wing tips, so that it could be brushed off before we would all launch into flight.

We were told about the tax-free lands that local kings showered on the Brahmins: *archanabogam*, *brahmadeyam*, *iraiyilinilam*, *chaturvedimangalam*. Banned by holy books from using a plough and believing that all manual labour was disgusting and degrading and fit only for the lower castes, the Brahmins would sublet their land. Because what was deemed fit for the Brahmin was deemed fit for everyone who wanted to feel superior and everyone who wanted to dominate, the landowning Naidus and the landowning Mudaliars and the landowning OtherCastes started to avoid all manual labour, too. We were told that this aversion to manual labour was a defining feature of ruling-class behaviour.

We were told that Marx had written about this. We were told that because we worked with our hands, we were the working class. We were also told that because we worked, and because they hated work, they hated us.

That explained the separate wells and the separate graveyards and the separate streets. That explained why we had to stay out of the schools. That explained why we had to stay outside their homes. That explained why our homes were in the *cheri*, outside their villages. That explained why our people had been killed. That explained everything that required explanation.

*

When the month-long curfew was finally lifted, our party held a procession to mourn our dead. Kilvenmani became communism, communism became Kilvenmani. Green fields, red flags, black bodies: our every single step was taking us towards revolution.

Since the Paddy Producers Association decided that it was their turn, they held a rival procession to show their strength. They said that Pallan-Paraiyan peasants were ungrateful dogs. They said Pallan-Paraiyan peasants were parrots who repeated whatever was taught to them. They said Pallan-Paraiyan peasants were foolish enough to fall headlong into the well just because their friend had dug it. They said that the arrogance and affectation of drummers and gravediggers was a result of the Communists. They warned everybody to give up the dream that the sickle could find work after the landlords came to ruin. They said that peasant associations were mental asylums for the untouchables. They said that the labour unions were whorehouses. They vowed that a hundred men like Gopalakrishna Naidu would burst forth. They said a hundred landlords were willing to go to the scaffold. They warned that the world would witness a hundred Kilvenmanis.

We burned all over again.

*

They were asking for a fight that we could not give.

They claimed that we had killed their agent to avenge our leader. A Pakkirisami for a Pakkirisamy. They boasted how Kilvenmani had become a cremation ground even before his body reached the graveyard. They said our village had asked for its massacre by killing one of their agents.

Even as they made a big fuss of his death, they taunted us with our tragedy: what happens to the saucy chicken that comes into the kitchen on its own accord? It ends up in a curry. What happens to frogs that croak endlessly? They are silenced when snakes find them.

They rejoiced in the revenge, but we were held responsible for inviting death.

*

The gunshots are confirmed. It is not a figment of our imagination. The reports from the forensic labs reveal that the stains on Raman's loincloth came from his own blood. That night he ran – having last seen his wife and son enter the fateful hut – and ran and ran in a bid to save his life, fainting outside a cattle-shed. The serologists also see the red in Palanivelu's *veti*, Muniyan's underwear, Ratnam's towel, Kaliyappan's banian. Clothes that are red with fire, red with its tongues of flame, red as the River Cauvery in flood, red ochre as that river in haste, almost as red as spilled blood.

*

Like the forensic scientists, the police are also meticulous in their observations. Because it is a road to nowhere, their reports talk about gunshot wounds sustained by coconut trees. They talk of the height and dimension and marks seen on the trees. The trees cannot come to court, the trees cannot give testimony, the trees cannot depose, so they are spared the horror of being eyewitnesses.

The doctors ape the police. Doctor Kausalya Devi submits a tabulated report of the pellets that she finds in our bodies. She finds three gunshot wounds on someone's face and two on his chest and one in his neck but she cannot feel the pellets with her hands and she cannot remove them. She tabulates the other gunshot wounds, too. Name, number of wounds, location. The locations vary from the cheek to the eyebrow to the neck to the chest to the palm to the stomach to the left thigh to the right ankle. The table tells you how we have been sprayed with their shotguns.

It was easy for them to write of us. Big in the scheme of things, six measures of rice is a mouthful to them. They digested us easily. News of these police reports came to us. These are the light-hearted reports. Not like the sad post-mortem reports where these doctors are enacting the struggle to determine the gender or the age from a body that has been charred like a piece of wood.

*

Less than a month after this tragedy, another round of tripartite talks was held with the representatives of land-holders, agricultural labourers and legislators to revise the wage structure. Where the wage for harvest was four local measures for every sack of grain containing forty-eight measures of paddy, it became four and a half; four and a half measures became five; five measures became five and a half; five and a half measures became five and three-quarters; and six remained at six with no change. We knew nobody followed this agreement to the letter, that nobody would ever give us six measures. We knew what would happen if six measures were demanded.

When a Muslim *mirasdar* in Poonthalangudi acceded and paid six measures, there were calls for all landlords to follow suit. Demonstrations went on until all work in the fields came to a standstill. It was time to crack the whip, the landlords decided, and they brought in the police to put down the protests. The police – being more refined than their feudal friends – used wooden lathis instead of whips, and when it really got out of hand, they fired on the crowd. A striking peasant died, a sub-inspector the culprit. History was already repeating itself.

Another deal was signed. This new agreement was used to silence us, to quell our fears, to placate us because we had paid with our lives. This agreement also contained other standard conciliatory catchphrases: they agreed to allow the employment of outside labour after local labour had been employed. They made us agree that they would not be forced to employ *lazy*, *inefficient* and *recalcitrant* labourers, shorthand to denote Communist peasants. They agreed that disputes had to be addressed to a conciliation committee under the local tahsildar with two representatives of the landlords and two representatives of the labourers. To buy time, this settlement was proposed for the next three years.

We burst with rage but we know that the landlords live behind high walls where nothing can get to them.

*

Everything that has happened so far is held against us. Everything that is bound to go wrong is blamed on us. We know that the landlords never care about the agreements. They know that words on paper have a life only on the page. They know that nothing can bind them. They know that these words don't belong to anybody. They know that words are stillness, meant to arrest hostile action. They treat paper no more preciously than pubic hair.

During the harvest season of 1968, the landlords had hired the police to work for them. The police had come from their camp and provided protection. The landlords, under police protection, had used hired labour from other districts; they went from village to village and they harvested the grain. This was part of their scheme of starving us to death: to deprive us of any employment, to deprive us of any means of subsistence. They planned to harvest the grain themselves with the police dogs standing guard and the hired hands slaving away. They wanted us to stand and watch and weep.

We did not let that happen. The soil we had toiled upon owed us food.

Just as fish know the depths of water and snakes know the sound of drums, we knew these paddy fields. So, we took them by surprise, too. At night, we harvested the crop because the land was imprinted on our hands. Days later, they too took us by surprise. At night, they killed us because death danced on their breaths.

*

We are told that action will be taken and arrests will be made only if we agree to the terms of the police. We knew that there was no one to arrest the police who had allowed the landlords to carry out Operation Kilvenmani.

Someone said: Do what they say or they will do to us what they did to Chinnasamy. The police could do anything. One matchstick was all it took for the Malabar Special Police to burn Chinnasamy's moustache. It was not enough to take away our moustaches to show that they were real men. They went even further, killing us in custody, opening fire on our meetings. We had not suffered as much even under the white man's police.

Now, they construct our case according to instructions from the landlords and their politicians. Our testimonies are watered down, so that it appears as if we contradict ourselves and each other. Framing a flimsy case, the police prepare the ground for the landlords to have sufficient escape routes.

Then they turn their attention to nailing us. The *mirasdars* are furious after agent Pakkirisami Pillai's murder. They see his killing as an affront to their might, but they also see his death as their whip to crack down on us. It is a murder that will help them leverage the massacre. They order the police to fix us up in that single murder case.

That is why we end up in jail.

Twenty-two of us go to jail for two months after our village lost forty-four lives.

*

When we went to court, we heard that all the accused landlords were angry that this false case was being foisted on them. Twenty of them averred, in true son-of-a-shotgun fashion, that they did not own a gun, or a licence to hold a gun, or that any gun had been seized from them, or that they had surrendered a gun. Right away, all of them agreed that they were members of the Paddy Producers Association. They denied all knowledge of the fires. They had fireproof alibis.

There was something they submitted to the knowledge of the court: some of them had been away on the night in question. Some of them had been absent.

We saw that all the absconding whoresons had since returned and we could not believe our ears when we heard them lie.

That night, Gopalakrishna Naidu (the first accused), had dropped in at the local talkies to enquire about something and then he had been with the police; the third accused had been away to attend his sister's father-in-law's cremation; the fourth accused had gone to his sister's house forty miles away to get his stomach ache treated by a doctor in that town; the sixth accused had been at his father-in-law's house tending to his sick wife; the seventh accused had remained home; the ninth accused also had remained home, where a six-member gang with four grievously injured members sought shelter because they were being chased by a Communist gang, which had started throwing stones at him and he had started bleeding and his mother fainted as she was too shocked and then the police came and the gangs dispersed and therefore he never went to the scene of crime because it visited him; the tenth accused had been in another city tending to his sister's husband, who had been hospitalized after an accident that damaged his teeth; the twelfth accused was at the night show at the talkies and having heard of the incident had stayed over at a friend's house; the thirteenth accused went to visit his son studying in Porayar where he had taken ill because of the tiring nature of travel and returned on the subsequent day; the fourteenth accused was only an occasional visitor to his village as he had resided in Nagapattinam for the last decade; the fifteenth accused was under detention; the sixteenth accused had slept at his rice mill in Parappannoor as was his usual practice; the seventeenth accused had gone to another village for harvesting; the twentieth accused had stayed home in his village along with prosecution witness number forty-four; the twenty-second accused had gone to Palayapalayam; and the twenty-third accused had gone with the local panchayat president on an election fund-raising mission to Tiruvarur to meet Sundaram Iyer, in whose home they had spent that fateful night.

The police, who had provided their lorries to these killers that night, did not produce any evidence that contested the claims of these landlords. They were mute puppets in khaki uniform.

*

Sometimes the disease is the cure, sometimes the cure is another disease. The police filed a case against the landlords, but they also filed a case against us. Complaint and counter-complaint. We were angry that they had made out two cases: one for this side, one for that side; both for their entertainment. As if killing one agent of the landlords was equivalent to the killing of forty-four old men, women and children. Twenty-two of us became the accused in Irukkai Pakkirisami Pillai's single murder case. Twenty-three landlords became the accused in the Kilvenmani case. We didn't know, but that was how the law worked. Soon, we saw the agent's killing become a murder case, while the massacre was reduced to a connected arson case. We were sent to jail; most of us, in any case.

It seemed to us that we only had two options: go to jail, or go to the graveyard.

We try to paraphrase the court. We try to understand contempt. We understand that massacres need not legally be murders. We also understand that when circumstances change, the facts change.

The police had taken a dying declaration from Palanivelu. Since he had scraped through and survived death, he was now an accused in Pakkirisami Pillai's murder case. We realize that the law has stealthy claws; it sneaks up and catches the most unsuspecting person.

*

We heard that the state assembly has stood up in silence for a minute as a mark of respect to the forty-two (plus two, double silent) who died in Kilvenmani. Not only for our deceased, but also for three former members and two sitting members of the assembly who had also recently died. We think they would have stood up anyway, even if nothing had happened in our village. Their standing up and staying silent for a minute had nothing to do with us.

*

Back in the courtroom, we watched the landlords own up to their crimes.

They did so with practised ease. The first accused said he was fixed because he was the number one enemy of the Communists. The second accused said he was being framed because he was a close relative of the first accused. The fifth accused said he was being indicted in this criminal conspiracy because he was a public speaker who had successfully broken up the party's agricultural strike by making caste-Hindu labourers report to work. The sixth accused said he was being fixed as a result of similar successful intervention that earned him the enmity of the Communists.

The eighth accused, the eleventh accused, the eighteenth accused and the nineteenth accused were being made to face this accursed fate because, being petty land owners, they had worked in other landlords' farms for lower wages in defiance of the Communist call for a general strike. This was self-justifying scab talk.

Then the others admitted their guilt. The tenth accused believed that he was suffering because he had prevented us from grazing our animals on his land, the fourteenth accused believed that he was suffering because he was the first accused's brother, the fifteenth accused believed that he was suffering because he was the fourteenth accused's son, the seventeenth accused believed that he was suffering because he had appeared as a prosecution witness in another case against a couple of us, the twentieth accused believed that he was suffering because he had served as a prosecution witness in many cases against us.

They were giving themselves up. They were making it clear that they were our enemies. We were happy with their honesty. But the judge pretended not to grasp the obvious, he bought into the victimized image peddled by the *mirasdars*. If they said they were our enemies, would that not explain why they would have attacked us and burnt our families alive? Why did the Special Additional First-Class Magistrate not understand this?

We did not know how the law worked. Of course, ignorance of the law was no excuse. But we did not know why this judge refused to see the truth when it was staring him in the face. We did not know how to make these thoughts penetrate his frozen skull. We knew that even poking his brain with a cattle-prod could not help him. He seemed to be perpetually drunk. Those books in his room were as useless as fifty sickles hanging around the hip of a man who did not know how to reap.

*

When heavy rains have passed, drops of water continue to trickle down the roofs of our thatched huts. That is how we felt when the police told the court that all three of the shotguns seized from the landlords were found to be in working condition by the forensics department. Muthusamy said that more than twenty guns were used that night alone, but we were happy that even small things were working in our favour. Everything would point to the criminals.

Then, the police said that the time of last use could not be ascertained at all.

A half-truth is not a lie, it is a long, long rope. When the guilty get a grip, they climb out.

*

At Muthusamy's tea stall, newspapers told us about a defeated censure motion.

'This House censures and disapproves the policy of the Ministry in particular respect, namely its failure to protect law and order in Tanjore district, resulting in the ghastly incident of arson on 25 December 1968 in the village of Kilvenmani and the death of 42 innocent women, children and old men.'

The newspaper also tells us that the motion was defeated 36 to 125, but that doesn't matter. A margin does not make a defeat in our name any better.

*

Soon, the government appointed a commission. It was called the Commission of Inquiry on Agrarian Labour Problems of East Tanjore District. Everyone called it the One Man Commission. Everyone said the commission was a paper tiger. Someone said it was a joke. Someone else said it was eyewash.

We went to the commission and repeated our stories. The party also sent a memorandum briefing the commission about the history of agricultural reform in East Tanjore.

The commission gave its report the following August. It found the wages to be a pittance. It said the wage had to provide for minimum subsistence. It recommended a wage revision once every three years. The government tabled the commission's report on the floor of the House. Nothing happened after that. Neither to the commission nor to the agrarian labour problems of East Tanjore district. We forgot the commission and the commission forgot us.

*

Less than a year after the horror, children started to die in our district. In the beginning, it was a story from somewhere else, but then it became an everyday occurrence. The newspapers claimed these were mystery deaths. It was a mystery to people who did not know about starvation. Only the children of the toilers and coolies died, not the children of the landlords or the children of the shopkeepers or the children of the teachers. The newspapers did not notice this detail.

We did not have any children to lose to death, because childhood has gone away from our village. Strangely, we have outlived our parents and our children. We live between the dead. The children who have survived sound like our parents.

*

We told our stories to the court and to the commission. We testified on their terms. We were examined and cross-examined. In their words, we deposed. Since we saw with our eyes, we spoke about what we had seen. However, the Special Additional First-Class Magistrate was not very pleased with our versions.

Perhaps he wanted a single story: uniform, end to end to end. The '*Once upon a time, there lived an old woman in a tiny village*' story. Sadly, we are not able to tell such a story. A story told in many voices is seen as unreliable.

In order to put us down, he quotes a big book. The big book quotes another big book. And it says, 'Unless the testimonies of two or more witnesses corroborate, it will not be possible to verify the guilt of the accused.'

We were men who were running to save our lives. We carried a different death in each eye. We cried. Our conches blew into deaf ears. They could see that the stories did not match. So the guilt would not be verified and the court would let them be, set them free. This is how the accused would be acquitted, this is how the guilty would turn innocent.

We were bound to lose. Because we do not know how to tell our story. Because we do not rehearse. Because some of us are tongue-tied. Because all of us are afraid and the fear in our hearts slurs the truth in our voices.

*

Hesitating would be of no help. We had made fools of ourselves with our speech and sloppy storytelling. Our silences made us traitors. We knew we had to fight. Fighting would bring us back to our right mind.

So, the poster wars continued and Keevalur's Chakravarti Press fattened on our hatred for each other and our love for catchy slogans.

The next season, we formally called for a strike. During the time of harvest, even a rat has five wives. It is the time of the year when we find a voice, when we can ask for more. The farmhands are few and fields have to be reaped in a day, or two at the most. Landlords dread the overcast skies that could drench the paddy and damage their livelihoods. They spend sleepless nights, thinking of calamities that could befall them if they fail to act on time. They fear strangers from half a dozen villages away harvesting the entire crop by night, leaving the field as ravaged as a raped woman. It is the only time of the year when their arrogance climbs down its long ladder.

Because life had to go on, they agreed to a round of talks because they needed us now more than ever. Even the state stepped in to provide machinery for the settlement of their disputes. But the landlords thought of our gain as their loss, so they never yielded ground. The three-cornered talks went in circles.

*

The prime minister of India was to come to our state. The DMK government begged the Central Government to give 100,000 tonnes of food grain in aid, preferably rice. That is what the newspapers said. Preferably rice. It was nice when the newspapers got these tiny details right.

We did not know if the 100,000 tonnes came. The newspapers forgot to write about that part of the story. In any case, we did not see the rice. In any case, it does not befit a starving man to ask the price of rice. We had seen our share of community inter-dining events, so we knew that what went by the name of a free lunch had a taste and an after-taste: spit of a mad mob, slag of its slur words, sour blood on a violent afternoon. Our hunger, accustomed to die on the mat, knows not to ask too many questions.

After the famine years, our state's budget could not make its ends meet. The Central Government said it would refuse to allow our state to present a deficit budget. The newspapers reported that the states had been warned not to overdraft or overdraw from the Reserve Bank. We felt that the country and states and the cities were no different from us. They were all villagers: some of them were land-lords and some of them were peasants. Like us, some states were running in debt. Like us, they were lining up for help. Like us, they suffered under bad moneylenders. Like us, some states had no escape. Pledged for a pittance, we knew that our loans would outlive us. We assume that they too are aware of such simple truths.

*

Like newspapers that wrote that we had set fire to our own huts, we know that cinema is also a lie. We know that cinema changes the truth: it takes our eyes by the arm and shows them around. It can conceal and reveal, it can rush at speed or crawl in slow motion. It can show demons entering a home by breaking through a tiled roof; it can show a man riding a flying lotus to meet a god and his wife in the clouds. Cinema loves the courthouse because it is full of drama and dialogue, because it is a chance for the lie to become the truth.

Cinema comes into our case too. Two men who run the Thevur Rajarajeswari Touring Talkies come into the picture. Chellaiyan. Chellamuthu. They give evidence of having seen Gopalakrishna Naidu when he dropped in at the cinema tent on the night of the incident at 8.30 p.m. The timing was during the interval, they say. The rest of the picture remains there, waiting to be seen. According to Chellaiyan and Chellamuthu, Gopalakrishna Naidu came by car. He spoke with them for five minutes and then went away. He had asked them if they were aware of the clash at Kilvenmani. He had asked them if they had seen Harijan gangs passing by. Chellaiyan and Chellamuthu had replied that when it had started to darken, they had seen some Harijans going to bury a body. Gopalakrishna Naidu then left the place. Chellaiyan and Chellamuthu add that the police head constable came later and made more inquiries. When asked under oath, the head constable remained loyal to the same story.

When the landlord drives a car, many cinematic events unfold. On that fateful day, when Gopalakrishna Naidu was variously spotted driving to and from Kilvenmani and Irinjiyur in his ash-coloured Ambassador, he stops at the cinema tent to enquire about a clash, he stops upon seeing the police lorry and offers to help, he gives money to Mrs Porayar to look after the medical expenses of her injured husband and son, and so on.

The court sees the picture as the landlords have painted it. But the picture in our minds is different. *Aadugal nanainchadhu enru onaai aludha mathiri.* Here, the jackal weeps because the goats are getting wet in the rain. Here, the jackal weeps because the goats are on fire.

*

On the night of the tragedy, the Rajarajeswari Touring Talkies was showing the movie *Vivasaayi*, where MGR played the role of a humble farmer to perfection. In the course of two and a half hours, the hero milked motherhood out of Tamil women, tamed a lipstick-and-frock-wearing English-speaking Tamil shrew, ran an agricultural research laboratory that contained innumerable varieties of grain, repaired tractors and settled disputes, handed over the surplus paddy from his farm to the government, prevented his father from switching to cash crops, saved the shrew's honour by saving her from a field-hand ready to rape her, saved his father's life, saved his father's potential killer's life, forgave his enemies and traitors, excelled in exhibiting his fighting prowess, and sang continuously about the importance of being a farmer.

*

Paddy smuggling became the new highway robbery. Sometimes the policemen would fight smugglers. Sometimes they would overpower them but often these gangs overpowered the police. Sometimes the police would take a bribe and allow them to escape.

Sometimes, the rice-mill owners pose as government rice-procurement agents and they cheat the landlords. Or this is what the landlords claim; maybe there is a nexus between the mill owners and the landlords, and together they cheat the government. They always figure out new ways to steal.

First we heard it happen, then we saw it with our own eyes, and then it was in the papers and, after a year, we saw these scenes played out even in the movies.

*

Our party was fighting. When the monsoons failed, the party wanted loans to be waived by the government. When famine hit, the party wanted relief measures. The party was fighting on the streets and inside factories. The party was fighting on the floor of the House and outside mills. There were indiscriminate arrests and wide-spread harassment.

This struggle was official. The truth about the wages was something else. We knew about it, the landlords knew about it, the Communist Party knew about it, the government, which brokered these talks, knew about it. Whether we asked for five measures or six measures was only a re-instatement of rights. Every farm used a *mottai marakkal.* The harvest would be measured in a container that could hold five measures of rice, but the container to dole out the wages would hold only four measures. The scale used to pay the workers was smaller than the scale used by the landlords to take their own share. We wrote to the tahsildar to stop this practice, we complained to the party, we took it up during the talks. Nothing changed, really. They had new containers now, shiny ever-silver cylinders, but they knew how to cheat. But we knew we were being cheated and we were fighting against it. It would not take long to dismantle them.

*

The party builds a martyrs' memorial in our village. It is a single, red-hued stone sculpted in the shape of an eternal flame. The fire of communism was burning.

The fire spread. In Kilvenmani, we read about it in the news: the labourers seemed to have started striking every-where. The peasants were fighting in North Arcot, they were fighting in Coimbatore, they were fighting in Madurai. Spinning-mill workers were fighting, teachers were fighting, electricity board employees, bus drivers, drainage workmen were fighting. They observed strike ballots and lightning strikes and mass walkouts and absenteeism.

Everyday there were lockouts and sit-ins. We heard about the lathi charge inside the mills. We heard about police shootings inside factories. They often portrayed the workers as villains, but we knew these stories. The labour leaders were all placed under arrest. Workers died and we saw the red flag flying high. We saw the revolution was near. We were ready for anything, and we saw that they were ready for anything. We spoke about them. We shared these stories of revolution endlessly between us until the stories slipped through the sieves of our minds and other stories came to take their place.

*

It was our duty, so, when it was time, we went to court. We gave witness. We felt their flood of questions eat us away. We were interrogated. We were examined and cross-examined and dismissed. We were angry because we were made to appear like storytellers who had conjured this massacre out of our minds.

We knew that the lawyers did not really care. We could sense it in the manner in which they explained away things. They claimed to have devoted a great deal of their time towards this case, but the ultimate result was not in their hands. They blamed the police for drafting a weak case. They said that their vexation did not arise from the merits of the case, which were clearly in favour of the state, which was fighting on behalf of the dead, but from the lack of substantive evidence.

We knew that we could not bring back the dead to give witness. We knew that the landlords knew this too.

*

The landlords everywhere played a simple game. It was the game of Outside Labour. In South Arcot. Or East Tanjore. The newspapers supported the landlords. They spoke of the constitutional right of the landlords to employ whomever they wanted to employ. We were discredited because we had been hungry, hungry for an increase in our wage year after year. They said we were clamouring to be like them. They said we should never forget that the crow who attempted to walk like a swan never managed to mimic its grace, instead he lost even his natural gait. They asked us to remember our station. They said even hawks could not carry away the sky, so scavenger crows like us should not have lofty dreams.

The newspapers put down this antagonism to our arrogance. They mislead the public about us. They blame the famine conditions on our strikes.

*

Nothing frightened them as much as the realization that we had stopped being frightened of them. Everything angered them, so we were punished on the slightest pretext. They did not allow our funeral processions to step into their streets – our dead would pollute them, just as we would. They wanted our lives to never go beyond Pallaththeru and Paraththeru. This was the punishment for being born as Pallars and Paraiyars. So, when we demanded our rights, we had to face the boycott from the caste-Hindus.

Even if we walked ten miles in search of a new job, some petty employment for the day, they would not give us work. They would not sell us things in their shops. We had to find a way around everything. That is what we did even for the burial ground. We could not use their streets to carry our dead, so we had to walk through the fields. When three of our people died in a week, no, not here, but from the neighbouring villages, they had the police file cases against us. They said we had ruined 125 sacks-worth of paddy by walking through their rice fields. When we had a dying person in the ten neighbourhood *cheris*, we all died a little because of the fear. We did not fear the caste-Hindus alone. The police were always at their beck and call and we could face fresh prosecutions if we broke their diktat.

In the beginning, they stopped funeral processions when they reached caste-Hindu streets. Soon, they started posting policemen in our *cheris* if one of us fell very ill.

They said they did not want us to wag our tails. They said that every untouchable who disobeyed them deserved to die in something similar to Kilvenmani.

*

We were used to it: the silence and the shouting. The songs and the tears. Wet from all our weeping, we saw the world in a blur. Death had been here, but life went on deliriously, as if it had been set on fire.

We do not know where our quest for justice will end. But we know that the police or the prosecution do not represent us. Our hopes for justice lie with the judge who is busy reconstructing the events of that night and shuffling them into a sequence. We wait for the Special Additional First-Class Magistrate to ask questions on our behalf. We want him to ask the accused why not even one of the forty-two (plus two, silent) people were able to escape their death? We want him to ask why they were unable to come out of the hut? We want to ask why the Paddy Producers Association cut off all the escape routes if their intent had not been to kill? We want him to ask the accused if they were all deaf and how they missed the screams of the trapped people if their intent had not been to kill? We want him to ask the prosecution the reason behind their belief that the door of the hut was unlocked? We want him to ask the prosecution why none of our people walked out of the hut when it was set on fire if the door had been open? We want him to ask the prosecution what prompted these forty-two (plus two, silent) people to commit collective suicide? We want him to ask the prosecution why did the police come to know about the deaths only the morning after? We want him to ask these easy questions. He does not ask these questions. He breaks into poetry and calls this incident heart-rending. He slips into mathematics and wonders how all the dead could have fitted into such a tiny space. He scrubs his conscience clean.

He is clearly not in a mood to ask our questions. He is the one who can ask them, not any of us. You see, even if the hen knows it is day, it is the cock that must crow.

*

An empty ground overlooks the Nagapattinam Court.

We converged there every day when the hearings were in session. We were patient. The waiting became the blood in our heads. To the lawyers, who had spent the greater part of two years working on the case, any judgment was gratifying. To the party, it meant more meetings, more denouncements, more discussions. To the eighteen bereaved families, the case was the shell they made their home, it was the hut where their loved ones had remained on the night of the tragedy. We were all waiting as the days dangled before us.

Two years after the atrocity, the Special Additional First-Class Magistrate M. S. Gopalakrishnan delivered his verdict.

He came to conclusions: the accused took the law into their own hands, deliberately set fire to the huts, destroyed all homes in three streets, shot at agricultural labourers. He doubtless grieves that their 'causing grievous harm' resulted in the loss of forty-two (plus two, silent) innocent lives and decides, in the circumstances of the present case, to impose a fitting punishment. He has a full meal in mind, but he skips the salt. He frees fifteen landlords. Eight of them get a token punishment of ten years in jail. No one is sentenced for life, no one is sentenced to death.

The Special Additional First-Class Magistrate also said that the accused who have been convicted by this Court of Sessions at the East Tanjore District on that the Thirtieth day of November Nineteen Hundred and Seventy should be handed over to the Tiruchy Central Prison.

Some issues are sidestepped. Most are buried. The court kept saying that the fire did the killing. At one point, the magistrate talked about the people who died because they were trapped inside a hut that caught fire. As if the hut of Paappa and Pandari Ramayya was waiting there, waiting to catch fire, waiting to self-immolate, waiting to commit suicide.

Our lawyers say justice has nothing in common with law. It is a late lesson.

*

The convicted landlords, already out on bail, announced their decision to challenge the order. When they went to the High Court, we laughed to ourselves. This was an old joke: for a minor stomach ache, a *mirasdar* had to run to Madras. Even there, the case dragged on and on for a further three years.

In the big city, we saw the final hearing of the case stretch for sixteen long days. Day after day, the judges would come and take their seats and listen to the arguments from both sides. The prosecution which was the police and the defence which was the landlords and then again the witness for the prosecution which was us. The judges asked question after question. Some of us who went there were already getting impatient. We wondered why they could never make up their minds. We marvelled at the words that came out of their mouths, always English, always in a steady tone, like a thresher at work. Sometimes, sitting in the court, grass grew within our heads and sometimes, we sensed snakes mating. Their English could shoot like darts, it could curl and coil around itself.

Muthusamy, who knew some English, would translate for us at lunchtime. 'They are talking about the massacre.' 'They are talking about seeing the massacre.' 'They are talking about what happened during the massacre.' 'They are talking about what happened after the massacre.' We stopped asking him for translations. Seeing their placid faces, we often had a feeling that nothing related to death was being discussed. 'How can they sit for so long in one place and silently listen?' asked Raman, and then he said, 'See, even my buttocks have fallen asleep on this bench.'

*

The state minister for agriculture was the minister of Harijan welfare – it was the government's way of acknowledging that we grew the food that everybody ate. These things went together, like gift and gratitude. Minister Sathyavani Muthu was like us, from one of the outcastes. This was their way of saying that even 'untouchable' people had come up in society.

The state was going to give us some money for our dead relatives. The state was going to support the voluntary organization that wanted to rebuild our homes. The organization had taken money from the refinery at Narimanam in East Tanjore and, because he still ruled over these villages, sought blessings and approval from Gopalakrishna Naidu. We reasoned it out by saying, 'Everyone who has taken on a body, has taken up a begging bowl.'

Years later, we think that it was a mistake. The landlords would show pictures of our new homes to the judges and claim that Gopalakrishna Naidu built them for us. The photographs would carry the lie to its logical end. All these acts of compensation and compassion cut deep into us.

These were knives that found every inch of our flesh. We were angry not only because we wanted to avenge the dead.

*

It is said that wisdom and learning are contained in a measure of rice. For our food, our fists fought the earth. For our freedom, our fists froze the air. Now, we saw them tamed by handcuffs. We spend our days in jail, eight of us ending up in prison for agent Pakkirisami Pillai's death. But the landlords, with blood on their hands, walk the streets with their heads held high. Congress leaders garland them.

Sadly, along the way, we see our party leaders use public platforms to please and provoke others. When Muthusamy went to Madras, he heard the Communist leader ASK Iyengar speak about the greatness of Prime Minister Indira Gandhi. 'She has nationalized banks and she has promised to eradicate poverty. We must support the Indian National Congress,' ASK said. We know that the Congress in Kilvenmani is not Indira Gandhi. It is Gopalakrishna Naidu. The politicians and the police are only puppets on his strings. We know it is a mistake to support the Congress.

*

When the Land Ceiling Act came, the landlords of Tanjore started their protests. They refused to pay land revenue, they refused to crop. They cried about the reforms. They asked to be exempted, and when it did not work, they started opposing the act. They figured out ways to work around it. Fraud would win where fights could not.

They grew used to complaining. They said they lacked proper transport facilities to take the levy paddy to the government warehouses, so they wanted the government to come and collect it instead. They fussed about little things. They behaved like moody, foolish cattle that require lots of cajoling. They established the right connections to the politicians to see that they were saved. Like vermin and rodents, they knew their way around. They were either members of the Indian National Congress or DMK, and because feudal funding fed these parties and kept them running, politicians took orders from *mirasdars*. Reforms and land redistribution, promised eloquently on paper, were never put into practice. They dug their way into every corridor of power, they worked to appropriate the voices that criticized them.

Even Periyar EVR, whom the entire state held in the greatest regard, who had vociferously condemned this massacre, was not out of their grasp. Patronage and caste connections helped them purchase proximity. We heard that Gopalakrishna Naidu had managed to meet Periyar when he had come to Nagapattinam and was receiving visitors at a school building. We felt let down. We found little to trust in Periyar's rhetoric of Self-Respect, the DMK's Tamil nationalism, or in the Congress promise to eradicate poverty.

*

While Indira Gandhi keeps making these promises, the shops run out of kerosene, the state runs out of coal. There is scarcity of petrol and diesel. There is a 75 per cent power-cut in Madras, the newspapers say. There is a 99 per cent power-cut in our villages.

Paddy is at nature's mercy. Failure of monsoons means drought and famine. Cyclonic winds means ruined crops. Excessive rain means rotten crops.

In between, the nation went to war with Pakistan. In between, there were reports of how the Naxalites were taking over the Western Ghats. There were reports of how the Naxalites were taking over the trade unions. Spinning mills were shut down. Factories were locked up. The country was in a state of emergency.

The Paddy Producers Association continued its crimes. Our party, as usual, opposed them. What one sought to do, the other sought to undo. Because the Communist Party held its meetings on new moon nights, the Paddy Producers Association held its meetings on full moon nights. That is how they behaved in every aspect. Often, we got drunk because we needed to stay tough. Between the bald heads and the braided tufts, there was little else any god could do.

*

Rumours, like bats, reached the remotest places. Someone said, 'Gopalakrishna Naidu's elder brother's son is getting married to the daughter of the brother of a judge of the Madras High Court.' Someone said that advocate Seshappa Iyer was responsible for this match-fixing. Our fate was sealed.

Even without the marriage we had little hope. The court in Tamil Nadu's capital city was nowadays known as the Tamil Naidu High Court. The chief justice was a Naidu. Seventeen landlords involved in that case were Naidus. They had all been represented by Thambaiah Naidu. We were all untouchables in their eyes. Listening to our case was going to be a ridiculous, empty gesture. The accused would enjoy justice as a favour.

We try hard not to lose the little hope we have.

*

The Madras High Court outdid Gopalakrishna Naidu.

Justice Venkataraman and Justice Maharajan argued that if the main intention of the mob had been to cause hardship to Kilvenmani, they should have torched all the huts in all the streets on which we lived. Because only the huts on one of the streets were set on fire, they concluded that the attack was retaliatory – to avenge the death of agent Pakkirisami Pillai – and not deliberate. We consoled ourselves that we were lucky that these judges were not part of the mob that rampaged through Kilvenmani.

Letters of Gopalakrishna Naidu to the chief minister were quoted word for word in the judgment to prove that he had been implicated in this massacre only because he was an enemy of the Communists. The judges held that we had found it difficult to contain our urge to make him the villain of this episode.

This court rejected all our testimonies. They found everything we said to be faulty, unreliable, contradictory, smacking of falsehood, lacking in credibility and an afterthought, so they refused to accept any of it.

The High Court judges were defending the landlords better than their defence lawyers. As experts of ruling-class behavior, they used their understanding of caste and feudal practices to bail out all the accused.

Muthusamy translated their judgment for us. It said: 'There is something astonishing about the fact that all the twenty-three persons implicated in this case should be *mirasdars*. Most of them are rich men, owning vast tracts of lands and it is clear that the first accused, Gopalakrishna Naidu, possessed a car. Such *mirasdars* might have harboured cowardly thoughts of taking revenge on Communist agricultural labourers. However much they might have been eager to wreak vengeance on the peasants, it is difficult to believe that they would walk bodily to the scene and set fire to the houses, unaided by any of their servants. Owning plenty of lands, these *mirasdars* were more likely to play safe, unlike desperate, hungry labourers. Anyone would rather expect that the *mirasdars*, keeping themselves in the background, would send their servants to commit the several offences which, according to the prosecution, the *mirasdars* personally committed.'

Though we had slaved on the fields of these Naidu *mirasdars*, we did not know that they could be capable of rage but incapable of revenge. We learnt it from the High Court. The judgment also said: 'It is truly regrettable that the forty-two agricultural labourers who sought refuge in the hut of Pandari Ramayya lost their lives because that house was set on fire. However, it is a little comforting to learn that the accused did not have any intention to burn them to death.

'In our opinion, the onus for responsibility of the tragic incident that took place on the night of 25th December 1968 lies with the accused, who have to accept the blame. But we regret the fact that we have not found sufficient evidence on record to implicate the accused in this incident. We have tried our best to separate chaff from grain, to lengthen the punishment for at least a few of the accused, and at the same time to ensure that the witnesses depose in a natural manner. But the subliminal shortcomings of the prosecution witnesses prevented us from punishing individuals whom we consider innocent. We believe the dependants of those who lost their lives in the holocaust will be generously compensated by the government.'

All the accused were acquitted. All of them walked free.

The fire of Kilvenmani had been rekindled. We were burning with outrage.

We told them that we did not want compensation.

We also did not want their justice.

EPILOGUE

* * *

Before this text is wrapped up and the book is mercilessly put down for being postmodern, here is a parting dose of Derrida: 'The book is the labyrinth. You think you have left it, you are plunged into it. You have no chance to get away. You must destroy the work. You cannot resolve yourself to do so. I notice the slow but sure rise of your anguish. Wall after wall. Who waits for you at the end? No one...'

This direct address startles you. You. You, unable to leave a book. You, plunged in its text. You, seeking to destroy the work. You, you, you. Seduced into this labyrinth, with no means of escape, you prepare yourself for the immense task.

Wait. What if you don't want to take it up? What if you decry deconstruction? What if you believe Derrida is a fancy French philosopher whom only the snooty guys at university quote? I am with you. So are most of the others. We are in this together. We are the 99 per cent. Come and occupy the novel, dear reader.

You, being this you, you being no ordinary reader, you being the collective, you being the reader who rights the wrongs, you being the reader who fills in the blanks, you being not only evasive but also anonymous, enter this story.

You have done all the preliminary groundwork. You know well that between the closure of the book and the opening of the text, there will be moments of wandering. You are prepared for the travel, the trials and the tribulations (you can ignore my alliteration). You have discovered much more than I stopped to say. You have studied beyond survey tabulations and statistical manipulations. You know, for instance, that the global market-economy made Tanjore a mono-crop region. You know that rice production under the colonial capitalist mode increased five times more than the population, but the working people's standard of living went on a downward spiral. You know all the strengths and sell-outs of communism in this dead-flat delta district. You know the trappings of agrarian resistance, you know the failings of a Tamil woman writing an English novel. You, being the perceptive reader, even know the history that I have glossed over. You don't take long to fault me for talking only about the white imperialists – you can quote someone's story that at the end of the eighteenth century, Hyder Ali's marching armies, aided by the French and Dutch, forcibly took away 12,000 children from Tanjore to Mysore. You know that at that time, men were massacred and that the unmentionable happened to women and only those who escaped into the forests survived. You even speculate on the *mookkaruppu por*, where invading soldiers were said to have cut off the noses of the masses and collected them in sackfuls. You can reel off the dates of self-immolation of thousands of women of the Nayak royalty to save themselves from the fate that awaited them at the hands of the Marathas. You are not afraid, you are not the self-censoring kind, you point out that the Marathas spoke Marathi, the Nayaks spoke Telugu, and for a long, long time, Tanjore was never ruled by the Tamils themselves, and even if they got to rule, who would have had power but the feudal landlords? You can skip the soft-pedalling, you do the hard talk. You will get away with it. You have courage, dear reader, your words will never cost you a career.

Armed with all this knowledge, you visit Kilvenmani. You want to get the atmosphere right. You want to get the season right. You go there during harvest time, you go there in December, on the first day of the Tamil month of *Margazhi*, when dew begins to diamond the golden fields, you select a Sunday, you avoid the crowds and Christmas rush, you go there ten days in advance of the anniversary of the massacre.

You go and meet Maayi, you want to measure up the old woman in my novel against the original one, you want to know if justice has been done to her. She is busy

– this is the harvest season after all, she has to earn her daily wage. You curry favour by telling her about your visit to Tharangambadi – Tranquebar for the Danish – her birthplace, her mother's home. You have touched her at a tender spot. She reminisces about her wedding, about the day she left her coastal village, about coming to Kilvenmani as a bride. Things were bad in Tharangambadi, but she had no idea that Kilvenmani would be worse. She shares her shock at seeing that her wedding feast consisted of nothing but pumpkin fry, a dried fish curry and rice. *Burma arisi.* Tanjore grew the best rice in the world, but Maayi and people like her were slaves and were fed second-grade food, the cheaper Burmese rice. When the British left, the coarse rice vanished too, and in the years of monsoon failure, or cyclones, famine ate up the people.

You like her metaphors. You see that she speaks in the style of all old women, her words slur because of the absence of teeth, all her consonants are flattened as they roll out of her mouth and her vowels seem no different from each other. You find it easy to understand because she speaks of the familiar and she speaks with emphasis and her hands dance as she speaks and everything fits itself perfectly into the grand story that she is weaving. Her hands tell you of how she, and other women from the *cheri*, could not take water from the wells or the lakes, how she had to wait for a caste-Hindu woman to take pity and pour water into her pot. She tells you that before petrol or *christoil* made its appearance, the coal-powered buses did not let the people of the *cheri* sit with the Hindus. In the cinema tents, she says, they were made to sit separately.

She shows how it looks, a *serattai*, the coconut-shell that the untouchables had to carry to the tea stall because they were not served in tumblers. Her husband had joined the Communists because they fought for these rights. Reeling under the spell of the Self-Respect Movement and the enticing militancy of early Communists, the people of the *cheri* had got together, entered the caste-Hindu village and dismantled the temple chariot. Word got around that Sannasi, her husband, had masterminded this protest. He was abducted one day, never to be seen again, until his body turned up two weeks afterwards, a hundred villages away. She beats her breasts, she weeps.

You stay silent for some time. You console her with stories of worse atrocities you have read about. She tells you that she does not know what is in those books you speak of. She has never gone to school. She tells you that caste is about having one set of people to read books, one set of people to be crooks, one set of people to misbehave, one set of people to slave. Impressed with you, she tells you that the young people of today have not seen anything. *Yes, they saw things like beatings, killings, police shootings, meetings but they did not see what these eyes have seen. Women were always stripped bare before they were beaten. Yes, yes, I am telling you the truth. These eyes have seen that, these eyes just as they see you today. The landlords, those great souls, would not bear the sight of seeing clothes tear. Poor women, they shrivelled in shame. The ones who died from the beatings were silently buried. The ones who survived swallowed their shame and some poison. What could we do? What could be done? We beat our breasts, we wept. And so it went.* Since food was followed by drink, *saanippaal* would be waiting for the beaten woman or man – cow-dung mixed in water – a concoction that would drain them to death. When the Communists came with their red flag of resistance, hoarsely shouting and leading strikes, this revolting practice was put to an end. She traces the history of feudal torture: being forced to drink diluted cow-dung was soon replaced by being forced to drink a cocktail of fertilizer, so disobedience brought no disgrace, but death.

Seeing Maayi garnering all the attention, the women of Kilvenmani gather around you. You ask their names, you remember their stories and you, being the people's person that you are, easily forge a conversation. You unravel them masterfully, telling them of a friend who lost a daughter, a sister who suffered sexual violence, and they talk to you in turn, filling you in with bits and pieces of other storylines. You learn of Veerappan's little daughter, who had unaccountably stopped speaking and, because the words had left her, nobody knew what had made her stop. She died in the fire, and the memory of one night of rape and terror that she carried in her died that night. And because you probe, you also learn, dear reader, that Kunjammal lost her infant when an insect fell into the cradle – the child had wriggled, cried in pain and, scratching herself, had fallen face-down into the mud and suffocated. When Kunjammal went to feed the child, she came to an empty cradle, and the women stopped work and began singing dirges. They tell you stories and stories in this manner, of women who do not appear here, of children whose names are not printed on these pages. Constrained by this text and its subtext, you lose those threads.

Move ahead and march forward, dear reader. You are wanted in so many places. You haven't even met the men yet. I understand your compulsions. You want to follow a certain structure, stick to the semblance of some discipline.

Have you entered a paddy field at transplantation time? One foot in the silt, you think the other foot will help you break free, so you shift your weight, and that leg sinks too. You cannot come away unless you are knee-deep in trouble. That is how it is with the women who have started sharing their stories: one thing leads to another, and it goes on in endless circles, one foot down, the other follows, and then it is just wading through the mud, and it is difficult to walk away. You are evidently in a hurry, and as you make no effort to hide the fact, the women volunteer to walk you to where you want to go. They show you the martyrs' memorial where Pandari Ramayya's hut once stood, they point to the forty-four names, they take you to the tree where their village made its fatal decision to stick to the red flag. You can spot the coconut trees riddled with gunshot wounds; you can recreate the night from your readings.

The women make it easier for you. They tell you that the rice fields were not the dwarves that you now see in front of your eyes. In the sixties, the fever of Green Revolution was only catching up, so the old rice varieties were still around and these grew as tall as ten-year-old children – spraying them with pesticide was very difficult because of their height – and men and women and children who took shelter in these fields on that night were spared because they could not be spotted. The fields are golden and ripe for harvest, the women entreat you to taste the rice. They pull the ears of paddy, peel the husk, and the grains of rice they give you are milky in the mouth. You thank them profusely, you thank them politely, and you keep at it until they ask you, '*What next? What else?*' and you tell them, diplomatically of course, that you want to meet Nandan, little Nandan from Part Three, Chapter Nine, the angry young Nandan of page 210. Word is sent, and tiny messengers tear across the village, but he is nowhere to be seen. You then ask about the other eyewitness you have encountered in the last 52,000 words, and a kid who went looking for Nandan remembers seeing Ramalingam at Muthusamy's tea stall, so you go there.

Over a glass of tea, you let the men know where you are from and what you do for a living and why you are here and when you plan to leave. You tell them of your fascination with the history of their village, you tell them where your sympathies lie, you make it clear that you have been heartbroken ever since you learnt of the Madras High Court judgment that absolved all the landlords. You share the people's anger, you make it known, in no uncertain terms, that the absence of evidence does not constitute evidence of absence. Even if you may not stand with the red flag, you tell them that you stand with the oppressed people, that you salute their struggle. You tell them that women and children didn't deserve to die. In turn, Ramalingam tells you that killing of children is a caste-Hindu specialty. He talks of the time when the people of the *cheri* built a hut where they met at night and learnt to read and write; of the witch hunt that followed, of a one-year-old child who was trampled to death by the landlords and the police because they could not find her father who was the Communist Party's first point of contact in that *cheri*. Even running away did not help, he says, because when the man came back from Burma or Singapore or wherever, he was dragged to the landlord's place and beaten to death. When

Ramalingam's uncle returned in disguise, he was identified. They pounded him to a pulp, poured kerosene over him and set him on fire. The police obliged the landlord by covering up the case and attributing his death to a fire that destroyed all the haystacks in that farm.

Ramalingam speaks non-stop, his sentences sprout without an end in sight – *you see*, ingadhaan, *you know*, ayyayyo, *what can I say*, adhu mattuma, *of course*, enna nadanthadhu, *you will agree with me*, indha aniyayathukku oru alavae illa – so you hear about how the mother-fucker *mirasdars* played the people of the *cheri* one against the other, Pallars versus the Paraiyars, even as you hear about the cinematic rivalry between MGR and Sivaji Ganesan. You hear about barbers desisting from offering their services to the people of the *cheri*; you are shown how the men fashioned shaving devices by inserting blades into flattened metal cylinders that held incense sticks; you learn that the only recourse to medicine was the *Anjal Aluppu Marundhu*, a cheap herbal powder for pain and fever and chills and cold. You learn that his life's ambition was to be in the army, that, in his time, studying up to the fifth standard enabled men to join the military, but that became impossible because he had dropped out of school for two whole years when his teacher started calling him 'Danger' for daring to wear red to class one day. You are told that it was forbidden for the people of the *cheri* to catch the eye of any caste-Hindu: they were made to hold their gaze to the ground. You see a demonstration of how prostration had perfected itself over the years, how men and women and children of the *cheri* were made to fall at the *mirasdar*'s feet, until the practice ingrained itself and people fell without hesitation, like palm trees severed at their roots. He goes on and on.

You listen carefully, you ask the appropriate questions. As an extravagant witness who has observed marital discord and military disasters with an air of appreciable nonchalance, you lend an atmosphere of everyday, even as you try to prise information from one of my old informants. You talk about a triple murder elsewhere in Tamil Nadu where unknown assailants killed a landlord and his two sons and left their three heads on the doorsteps of his bungalow. Your questions follow: '*Is there Naxalite activity here, have they talked of eliminating their class enemies? Annihilation? Assassination? Do they spread their propaganda through their secret meetings? Did they compile a charter of rapes and murders and lawlessness to show why a landlord is an enemy of the poor and landless peasants? Have they held a people's assembly in your village?*' How can you falter in this fashion, dear reader? Are you not aware that the more you ask, the less they will speak, and that sometimes you have to shut up in order to prevent rousing people's suspicions? You might speak their language, stay in their homes, sleep on their mats, but people keep their secrets wrapped up. We might share this page, but beyond the careless chatter, I don't know what your political affiliations are. Who knows who you work for, to whom you owe allegiance? Maybe you work for the Q Branch, the state intelligence. Maybe you work for Naxalites, harping on about a new democratic revolution, a dictatorship of the proletariat and driving out the class enemies from the countryside by means of liquidating landlords and sustaining the guerrilla struggle, and all this questioning is simply a charade to hide your identity. In any case, the people will not help you in combing out the truth.

Now an uncomfortable silence prevails, everyone dismisses your suggestion of people taking the law into their own hands; they pooh-pooh your suspicions of Naxalite activity.

I am confident that you are capable of salvaging any situation, dear reader. You break the impasse by bringing up talk of the Gypsy Goddess. They attest to the legend, they repeat the story of seven mothers who were burnt to death, along with their many children; they tactfully point out that the temple exists in Pudukkottai, which is a part of Tanjore, but much farther away. They reassure you that their village has its own guardian deity. They take you there.

At the Kali temple, there is a feast of *sakkarai pongal* cooking. You ask the people for the occasion, for any reason for this celebration, and they laugh an open, whole-mouthed, belly laugh, and tell you that this day is special because you have come to their village. The more you infantilize them, the more they treat you like a child. Some conversations are closed on cue, and knowing that there is no point in probing further, you make it known to the people that you want to go to Irinjiyur, Gopalakrishna Naidu's village.

Feigning interest in the cause of dear old balance and self-screwed neutrality, and the latest fad of ethical journalism, you reveal that it is solely in your professional interest to secure his interview. 'My visit would be pointless otherwise,' you say, and everybody understands that the amateurs always have it hard. Dear reader, they also understand – given the timing of your visit and the circumstances under which it has been facilitated – that this is one of those 'anniversary special' stories that you are working on, that, twelve years on, Kilvenmani is a season-ticket for journalists who want to make a pilgrimage into people's memory, that writing an annual one-page article salves not only your conscience, but also everyone else's. You are allowed the privilege of being seen as progressive, the system is allowed the pitfall of being problematic, and the people – potent enough to pay back – are promised paradise for staying pathetic. (Forgive the former alliterative sentence.) Back to you, dear reader, dear reader. Back in the village of Kilvenmani, back on the fourteenth day of December 1980, back on that lazy Sunday, when you express your intent to meet Gopalakrishna Naidu with the most honourable of motives. The villagers smirk and laugh, they elbow one another and tell you that, yes, yes, you should go, that today is the perfect day to see the head of the PPA.

You are taken to his Irinjiyur residence, where you are informed that today being the day of harvest, he is now at Anakkudi. You see his Alsatian on the last leg of its life, and for whose sudden ill-health suspicion has now fallen upon the cook – you do not catch his name, but he is the one who appears earlier in this novel – and he, fearing dismissal any moment, is too eager to please, so you press upon him the need to meet his master, you brandish your credentials, and, learning how well-connected you are – and knowing nothing about six degrees of separation – the cook sends word.

You impatiently wait in that house of many, many rooms when word reaches you that Gopalakrishna Naidu has been killed. At first, you do not believe the news of his death. You go to Kilvenmani to personally ascertain the facts of the assassination. You hear rumours of beheading. You hear rumours of forty-four parcels, each wrapped in palm fronds, sent to the people. But you shouldn't believe all that you hear and you shouldn't tell all that you believe.

You watch the women sing of the landlord's perverse lust, his bloodthirst and this red harvest. You hear the men say, with a sigh, '*Mudivu kandachu*,' which can be variously translated as 'It has been completed' or 'We have seen the end.' You join the people of Kilvenmani – on the village streets, in their paddy fields, in their toddy shops – as they rejoice in the revenge. You know, more than anyone else, how they have waited every day for this day.

Mudivu kandachu. It has been completed. We have seen the end.

Acknowledgements

A long list of thank-yous to:

Amma, for putting up with a moody rascal who happens to be her daughter. So far, she has only received heartache in exchange for her love for me. Appa, for listening to my never-ending outrage, for talking to me about the hunger and poverty of his childhood with a pain in his eyes that my words cannot capture, for taking me back to a reality that he had struggled hard to escape, for travelling with me on every trip to Tanjore, for sleeping with my manuscript by his pillow, for his secret pride. Thenral, for hugs and massive financial helping-out and sisterly motivation that involves constantly teasing me for having these dream projects, and for promising to read this novel only when it is finally, properly, decently published. Cédric Gérôme, for being the love in my life.

The many places, apart from home, where this book was written. The International Writing Program in 2009 at the University of Iowa that afforded me the time and space to do my mandatory reading. The Charles Wallace Trust (CWIT) Fellowship in 2011 at the Department of English, University of Kent, where the first draft of this book was written. Alex Padamsee, for being kind enough to make time to allay my first-time novelist fears over cups of coffee. Richard Alford who runs the CWIT for selecting me for the grant, and to the British Council in Chennai for their help with this residency. Uma Alladi and Dr Sridhar for offering me a fortnight-long residency at the University of Hyderabad when I needed it the most. Bill Herbert, for hosting me at the University of Newcastle in the summer of 2011, and Debbie Taylor, for being an inspiration.

David Godwin, for almost being my third parent, for helping me pick up the pieces of my life, for pulling me back into writing when I thought all was lost. On some sad nights, I kept at writing not only for myself, but because I didn't want to fail you.

James Roxburgh, patron saint of Tamil mistranslations and the 24-hour clock, for the brilliant edits, for putting up with my endless procrastination, and above all, for what seems to resemble an unending conversation. You possibly know Kilvenmani better than me by now. Belinda Jones, my copyeditor, for not just spotting errors, but also politely pointing out when a village woman started appearing under another name towards the end of the book. Helen Crawford-White for coming up with a cover so retro, so flamboyant-camp-and-Tamil-and-1960s-all-at-once. Ravi Mirchandani, for deciding to run with this book, for not complaining about the many Camel cigarettes that I shamelessly snitched from him, for being so cool. V.K. Karthika, for publishing me in India and, above all, for taking a liking to this reckless, badass writing.

My friends in the United Kingdom for opening their homes to me, for countless meals and the welcoming space to sleep: Farah Aziz, Murali Shanmugavelan and Claire Sibthorpe, Sarah Sachs-Elridge and Senan, Sabitha Satchi and Seena Praveen.

Ajit Baral, Akshay Pathak, Amanda, Anne Gorrissen, Azad Essa, Ayesha, Isai Priya, Jaisingh Amos, K. Maariappa, Keerthikkan, Lekshmy Rajeev, Millicent Graham, Nikhila Henry, Pilar Quintana, Raphael Urweider, Ronelda Kamfer, Shazia Siraj, Sumana Roy – for support and advice and love, I cannot thank you enough. To Jaison, Jolly Chechi, Uma, Thushar, Jenny, Suja Bharathy, Prasanth, Ami and Thachukutti, Auswaf, Anver, Haseena, Hoda, Iza, Fatima, Diya, Noushad, Vinod, Sudhir, Asha, Tara among many, many, others, for making my visits to Kerala a home-coming.

Javed Iqbal for consoling me from far away, over GTalk, on a crazy winter night in 2009, saying that there is no story that cannot be told, and for adding that the difficulty in telling a tale is a story by itself. S. Anand, for wildly suggesting several years ago that I should attempt to write a non-fiction history of Tamil Nadu's worst massacre of Dalits to date. I was too shy to take up that challenge. Andy Barker, Sara Dickey and Ravi Shanker for their valuable inputs on early drafts.

Comrades in the Communist Party of India, Communist Party of India (Marxist) and the Viduthalai Chiruthaigal Katchi for their help in making it easier for me to reach the people and, therefore, their stories. Comrades A.V. Murugaiyyan, District Secretary of the CPI(M); A. Kumaresan of *Theekathir*, Kaaviyan and G. Ramakrishnan, for their moral support and standing by me. Comrade Balasubramaniyam at the CPI(M)'s Nagapattinam office for the classic full-timer's dedication.

Comrade R. Nallakannu, from the Communist Party of India, for being the hero of the working classes, for embodying simplicity and struggle, for always having a kind word for me. You are the leader I look up to. Comrades D. Raja, Tha. Pandian and C. Mahendran, for their help and support, for unfailingly asking me how the writing was progressing, for sharing anecdotes and archival material whenever I sought their help.

VCK leader Thol Thirumavalavan; translating his essays in the summer of 2003 first led me to read up extensively on this massacre. To him, I owe a great deal in learning about the extreme violence visited on Dalits, and the people's history of militant resistance. D. Ravikumar, whose writings have impacted the manner in which caste politics is understood, for encouraging me to write this novel.

Thevur Thangaraj for extensive interviews where we discussed the discreet perversions of Nagapattinam's landlords among other things. Chellamuthu, son-in-law of Kilvenmani's Muthusamy, for tirelessly retelling his story. Maniarasan, Kokoor Saravanan and Thangamani for taking me to villages in East Tanjore beyond the ones that concerned this particular novel. In Nagapattinam, A. A. Irudayaraj and Devadoss, for allowing me to use their offices as the unofficial point of initial contact. Justice Chandru for taking a trip down memory lane and recounting his field trips and his perception of the verdict.

Mayilai Balu's book *Ninru Kedutha Neethi* that exhaustively documents the judicial proceedings and the failings of the Kilvenmani story. Bharati Krishnakumar's documentary film *Ramayyavin Kudisai* that provides a reconstruction of the tragedy and lets survivors tell their own story. Tamil writer Appanasamy for guiding me towards textual sources, and for his splendid book *Thenparai Muthal Venmani Varai* that traces the history of feudal atrocities and resistance in the Tanjore district. Solai Sundara Perumal's novel *Sennel* and Pattali's novel *Keezhai Thee* – for skillfully maneuvering a long-ago massacre into the realm of fictional retelling. This novel owes a good deal to the back issues of *Janasakthi*, *Theekathir*, *Dalit Murasu* and *Thaaimann*, and the comrades who allowed me access to the wealth of information contained in those pages.

Researching for this book, I think in retrospect, was one of the ways in which I tried repeatedly to escape from the task of actually *writing* it. Yet, the research does put in an odd appearance here and there. The out-of-date devils in the first chapter owe their descriptions to Bulmer's research on demon worship in southern India published in 1894, the map at the beginning of the book is based on a limited-edition print from the Survey Office in Madras dating to 1905, the knowledge of the precise year of floods must be attributed to the Tanjore District Manuals authored by a Gazetteer named Hemingway. I don't want to show off any more. If anything, unlimited access to JSTOR (courtesy of Anna University) made me grapple with the fact that years of fighting and bloodshed could be flattened into three lines of class-warfare theory. I'm still getting my head around that.

This book belongs to the people of Kilvenmani. For making me their own. For the glass of water they offered every time I entered their homes. For asking nothing of me. For revisiting the most traumatic day in their memory. For having the belief that I would be true to their story. For their pride in standing by the red flag. For their faith in the idea of communism. For the enormous sacrifices they have made.

The many villages in Tanjore that I visited where the people treated me like the long-lost daughter that I think I am. For the people who stopped work to answer my endless questions and buy me cups of tea. For the women who let me work alongside them and taught me how to transplant paddy. For the dark and handsome young men on the fields, who spontaneously serenaded me with the classic MGR song, *naan paarththadhile aval oruththiyaiththaan nalla azhagiyenben nalla azhagiyenben...* It is almost impossible to resist such charm. When one drastically sheds the comforts of an insulated existence, it is small pleasures like this that make the search for a story so worthwhile.